Paul Doherty was born in Middlesbrough. He studied History at Liverpool and Oxford Universities and obtained a doctorate at Oxford for his thesis on Edward II and Queen Isabella. He is now headmaster of a school in north-east London and lives with his wife and family near Epping Forest.

Paul Doherty is the author of the Hugh Corbett medieval mysteries, The Sorrowful Mysteries of Brother Athelstan, THE SOUL SLAYER, THE ROSE DEMON, THE HAUNTING, and DOMINA, all of which have been highly praised.

'Paul Doherty has a lively sense of history . . . evocative and lyrical desciptions' *New Statesman*

'I really like these medieval whodunnits' Sarah Broadhurst, *Bookseller*

'Teems with colour, energy and spills' *Time Out*

'Vitality in the cityscape . . . angst in the mystery; it's Peters minus the herbs but plus a few crates of sack' *Oxford Times*

'The book is a pleasure to read and written in an uncompromising prose, the plot developed with intriguing twists and turns. Doherty's deep understanding of the period and the nitty-gritty of historical detail are to the fore without intruding on the rhythm of the plot. Superb entertainment' *Historical Novels Review*

'As always the author invokes the medieval period in all its muck as well as glory, filling the pages with pungent smells and description. The author brings years of research to his writing; his mastery of the period as well as a disciplined writing schedule have led to a rapidly increasing body of work and a growing reputation' *Mystery News*

A HAUNT
OF MURDER

The Clerk of Oxford's Tale of mystery and murder as
he goes on pilgrimage from London to Canterbury

Paul Doherty

<u>headline</u>

First published in 2002 by
HEADLINE BOOK PUBLISHING

First published in paperback in 2003 by
HEADLINE BOOK PUBLISHING

10 9 8 7 6 5 4 3 2 1

ISBN 0 7472 6075 3

Typeset in Times by Palimpsest Book Production Limited,
Polmont, Stirlingshire

Printed and bound in Great Britain by
Clays Ltd, St Ives plc

HEADLINE BOOK PUBLISHING
A division of Hodder Headline
338 Euston Road
London NW1 3BH

www.headline.co.uk
www.hodderheadline.com

To Mark Loster, first deputy of Trinity Catholic High School, for all his good work over the years.

The Prologue

The great raven, hooded and cowled like a monk, its broad ruff of feathers up behind its head, perched on the rotting post and croaked to the gathering night. Above it, crows, mournful in their cries, circled the fields, still searching for food before the sun dipped into the west. The pilgrims, weary and tired, now had no thought about the blessed shrine of St Thomas à Becket or praying before his consecrated bones. They were saddle-sore and weary with aching backs, chapped thighs, wrists tense from clasping reins. Sir Godfrey Evesden had ridden out and come back sombre-faced: once again they were lost!

The pilgrims turned and glared at the person responsible. The miller, drunk in the saddle, clasped his bagpipes like a mother would a child. The only sign that he was even conscious was the occasional burp or smacking of his lips. On either side the colic-faced reeve and the pimple-scarred summoner held him straight in the saddle. Sir Godfrey Evesden rode up. He was not frightened of the miller's great girth or his powerful fists which could pound a fellow like a blacksmith hammering a sheet of metal.

'You, sir!' He tugged at the miller's beard. 'You said this was the way!'

The miller opened his red-rimmed eyes and glared fiercely at the knight. 'Let go of my beard, sir!'

'Certes I will!' The knight let go then drew his sword. He brought its blade flat down on the miller's shoulder.

'We shouldn't have listened to him,' the friar piped up.

'Well, you did,' declared the yeoman, Sir Godfrey's loyal retainer.

It had all begun that morning. They had started out, merry enough with the sun rising and all refreshed after leaving St Botolph's Priory. They were on the road to Canterbury and the miller had announced in a booming voice that they would pass near Demonhurst Copse, reputedly one of the most haunted woods in Kent. Full of good ale and meat from the priory kitchens, the pilgrims had all demanded to be taken there. After all, wasn't the weather good, the sun strong, the trackways firm beneath their horses' hooves? Moreover, the carpenter's tale the previous night, full of ghosts, demons and sprites, had fired their imaginations. Matters had not been helped when they had stopped at the White Horse tavern and the miller had indulged in some tantalising tales about Demonhurst. Sir Godfrey had objected, so had his son, his pretty face framed by golden locks. The yeoman also had shaken his head but, led on by that imp of Satan the summoner and the gap-toothed, merry-faced wife of Bath, the pilgrims had taken a vote: they would spend that night at Demonhurst.

They had left the main highway and journeyed along the lonely, winding lanes of Kent. The miller, of course, had filled his wineskin at the White Horse only to empty it in generous slurps. He had lost his wits and they had lost their way. Now darkness was falling. A cold breeze had sprung up and where was Demonhurst Copse?

'By the rood!' the flaxen-haired pardoner screeched, pushing his horse up beside the knight's. 'You have led us a merry jig, you golden-thumbed rascal!'

The miller just belched. He would have maintained his surliness but Sir Godfrey Evesden's ice-blue eyes held his. A killing man, the miller thought, his fuddled mind now clearing; Sir Godfrey did not tolerate japes or jests at his expense.

'You have led us here, sir!' the knight hissed through clenched teeth. 'Night is falling. We are cold, we are hungry, we are saddle-sore.'

The miller turned in the saddle. He stared down the lane thronged with pilgrims jostling on their tired mounts. The taverner approached, confident that the knight would protect him from the miller's fierce rages.

'Sir Godfrey speaks the truth,' he barked. 'I did not welcome your suggestions, sir.'

'Shut up, you mealy-mouthed ale master!' the miller spat back. 'You wouldn't know a firkin from a cask or a tit from a—' Sir Godfrey's sword slipped nearer his neck.

The miller caught the reproving eye of the lady prioress seated on her palfrey, still clasping that bloody lap dog. Behind her was the pale-faced monk, cowl pulled up. He was the only one who took pleasure out of the chaos caused: red lips parted, those white, jagged teeth jutting down like a dog's! The miller shivered. He was frightened of no one but the monk terrified him – ever since Sir Godfrey had told that story about the blood-drinkers! Ah well, the miller concluded, it was time he showed these pious noddle-pates that he wasn't as drunk as they thought. He turned with a creak in the saddle and pointed across the great field to his left. Thrust up from the earth, like some Satanic pillars, stood a huge copse of copper beech, oak, sycamore, rowan and ash.

'Have a good look at that, you country sirs! See the many different varieties of tree? That's because it's ancient. There be Demonhurst Copse. I have brought you to it and Heaven help us if we spend the night there!'

The message was repeated down the line of pilgrims; they all stared across the field. The sun was now a fiery disc, casting out a strange, eerie glow. It lit the ploughed field and made the copse more threatening against the dark-blue night sky.

'Pray to the good Lord,' the man of law whispered to the franklin. 'Sir, perhaps this was not a good idea.'

'Do you think he's lying?' The franklin, with his snowy-white beard, adjusted the silken purse on his brocaded belt.

'I don't think so,' the man of law replied. 'Our miller may be sottish in his ways but he has sharp wits. I have heard of Demonhurst. But, come, it's either there or sleeping in the fields.'

Sir Godfrey had already found a gap in the hedge. Led by him, the pilgrims streamed across the field. The night air felt cooler away from the protection of the hedges and as they drew closer, the copse seemed taller, more forbidding. Sir Godfrey's hand fell to the pommel of his sword. His son came up beside him.

'Does it remind you, Father?'

'Yes, it does,' Sir Godfrey replied, his mind going back to those sombre, heavily wooded valleys of Transylvania and Wallachia. 'Devil's places' he had called them, sprawling forests of eternal night, which housed all forms of horror. Sir Godfrey's mouth became dry; he wished there was more sound from the trees.

The rest of the pilgrims hung back. Sir Godfrey urged his horse into a canter, a show of defiance against his own fears and theirs. Among the trees the undergrowth grew thick and rich but there were trackways through. Silent as the graveyard! Sir Godfrey cursed as an owl hooted high in the branches and his horse became nervous at the cracking and the snapping among the bracken. The trees were ancient, moss-covered; their branches stretched out, interlacing with each other as if in quiet conspiracy against the sky. Sir Godfrey turned in the saddle.

'Come on!' he shouted. 'This is where you wanted to rest, so rest ye will!'

Led by the squire and the yeoman, the weary pilgrims

entered this midnight place. All conversation died as if they wished to respect the hushed silence surrounding them. Sir Godfrey urged his war horse on. A skilled, trained animal, the destrier obeyed, although Sir Godfrey felt its muscles tense as if it was about to rear up and lash out as he had trained it to do whenever danger threatened. Here and there the trees thinned into small glades. A rabbit scurried across the path. Sir Godfrey's horse whinnied in protest and the knight leaned down and patted it gently on the neck.

'Now, now, sir.'

He looked to the left and the right. In places such as this in Wallachia and Moravia, those blood-drinkers, those creatures from Hell with their gargoyle faces, would spring an ambush. Sir Godfrey cursed; this was Kent, England's fairest shire, yet his mind kept playing tricks. He thought he glimpsed shadows flitting through the trees; on one occasion some grotesque half-animal seemed to crouch on a branch but these were only phantasms of the mind, tricks of the light on twisted wood.

'The forest of the damned,' the yeoman whispered. 'Sir Godfrey, how can we rest here?'

As if in answer, the trees thinned again to reveal a broad glade still lit by the dying rays of the sun. At the far end a small brook gurgled, the grass was green and high, lush fodder for their horses. Wild flowers coloured the ground: bogbean, primrose, field pansy, even some milkwort which, Sir Godfrey knew, shouldn't be blooming for another month. It was a quiet, tranquil place which brought cries of appreciation from his companions.

Mine Host urged his horse forward. 'We can sleep here.'

'Yes, we can,' Sir Godfrey agreed. He wished to impose order, drive away the terrors they had experienced since entering the copse. 'Come on now!' he called, clapping his hands.

Soon the glade was filled with noise and bustle. Sir Godfrey directed the pilgrims as if they were a troop of royal archers in enemy country. Horse lines were established. The yeoman took his sword and began to cut some of the grass. The miller, pardoner and summoner helped, piling the grass up. The horses were gathered and hobbled. The cook took a leather bucket and carried water along the horse line. Saddles were stacked, panniers, saddlebags arranged in a tidy heap. Fresh water was drawn from the brook for cooking and for washing. The glade was divided, one half for the women, the other for the men. Some of the men volunteered to stand watch.

The yeoman went out into the woods and, within the hour, he was back with three snared hares. The camp fire grew, providing light and warmth; a brand was taken and a smaller, cooking fire lit. The hares were quickly gutted, herbs picked and the glade was soon full of the savoury smells of cooking. Bread and wineskins were drawn from the common supplies, pewter and tin cups shared out. There were not enough traunchers to go round so some used great leaves or pieces of wood. The parson led the prayers, a hymn was sung and then the pilgrims sat in a circle round the fire eating the succulent roasted meat, their cups filled with ale or wine. Contentment flowed. The pilgrims relaxed, ignoring the tendrils of mist creeping through the trees into the clearing.

'We shall make an early start tomorrow,' Sir Godfrey announced. 'This is a place worth visiting but in future perhaps we should keep to the main highway.'

A murmur of assent greeted his words, particularly from the more venerable of his companions.

'It is an eerie place,' the pardoner declared in a high-pitched voice, wiping his greasy fingers on his jerkin and staining the relics which hung on a string round his neck. The fellow didn't care. He had tried to sell some of these tawdry objects but his companions had been unimpressed by his bags of so-called Papal Bulls, Indulgences, and various precious relics.

'Yes,' the summoner agreed, his mouth full of half-chewed meat. 'Why is it haunted?'

The miller burped, grasped his bagpipes and blew a long blast, a ghoulish, bone-jarring sound which awakened their fears. He lowered the bagpipes. 'Many years ago,' he began, 'when William the Norman came to England, the local fyrd—'

'What's that?' asked the wife of Bath, picking at her teeth.

'The local fighting men,' the clerk of Oxford answered.

Sir Godfrey glanced at him in surprise. The clerk was usually as quiet as a mouse. He wore a threadbare jerkin, patched hose and scuffed boots, and his cloak had more rents in it than it had cloth but he was neat and clean. His black hair showed early signs of grey and his shaven face always looked slightly sad. He constantly narrowed his eyes as if his sight was poor. A valuable copy of Aristotle's *Metaphysics* accompanied him everywhere.

'As I was saying,' the miller drew himself up, 'the local people rose in rebellion but the Normans crushed them with fire and sword. The survivors, men, women and children, sheltered here. Their leader went out with a cross to beg for mercy but according to the legends the Normans struck him down, charged into Demonhurst and butchered all the survivors here in this clearing.' He paused and stared over his shoulder at the gathering night. 'All butchered!' he repeated in a dramatic whisper. 'The grass was ankle-deep in blood. At night you can still hear their cries for pity, the terrible groans of the dying.' He leaned forward, his face like that of a gargoyle in the dancing firelight: popping blue eyes and red, spade-like beard. 'They say the corpses lie buried in this very glade, which is why the grass and flowers grow so lush.'

'We shouldn't have come here,' quavered the prioress.

'Oh, fiddlesticks!' the wife of Bath scoffed. 'I've stayed in more frightening places!'

'Do you think ghosts do exist?' the friar asked. 'I mean, Holy Mother Church preaches that when we die, we go to Heaven or Hell or wait in fiery torment in Purgatory.'

The pilgrims shifted and moved. The fire was bright, the sparks jumping up like souls escaping the very torment the friar had described.

'Well, we know there are ghosts,' the man of law declared importantly. 'Does not Holy Scripture relate how the Apostles thought Christ was a ghost when he came walking to them across the water?'

'True, true,' the taverner agreed. 'And some of the stories we have heard,' he smiled across at the poor priest sitting next to his brother the ploughman, 'have mentioned ghosts which are as real as the trees around us.'

'I wonder what they are like,' the reeve murmured. 'I mean, look around you, good pilgrims. Night has crept in. Darkness covers the face of the earth. But the mist . . .' An owl screeched and made them all jump. 'Is it really mist or the souls of those who died here?' The reeve nodded. 'I do wonder what it is like to be a ghost.'

'I can tell you,' said the clerk of Oxford, staring into the fire as if lost in memories.

'Now, there's a tale!' the miller exclaimed. 'I don't know about you, good sirs and ladies, but I am not yet ready for sleep. Will you tell us, sir?' He looked at the clerk. 'You know our custom? During the day a merry tale but at night one to chill the bones and freeze the blood.'

'Yes! Yes!' chorused the rest of the pilgrims.

The clerk stared across at Sir Godfrey. 'It is a tale of love and death and, yes, it may well chill the blood!' He eased his legs. 'And in this place I must tell you it and make my full confession.'

The Clerk's Tale

PART I

Chapter 1

Ravenscroft Castle stood on a small crag, a brooding, rocky presence not far from Blackwater River outside the town of Maldon in Essex. Ravenscroft had been built in an age when God and his saints slept, when Stephen and Mathilda waged relentless civil war. It was built for both defence and attack with a square donjon, or keep, soaring up to the sky, defended by a lofty curtain wall and rounded towers. A massive yawning barbican defended the gate which could only be approached over the drawbridge across a broad, stinking moat. Nevertheless, in the year of Our Lord 1381, Beatrice Arrowner, just past her seventeenth birthday, had no thoughts of war or strife. It was May Day, when all the townspeople of Maldon honoured the Blessed Virgin Mary, God's pure candle who brought forth the light of the world.

Maypoles had been set up on various greens. Troubadours

and troupes of travelling actors had arrived, and stalls and booths had been erected on the common land. Oxen, pig, hare and pheasant were being roasted over spits turned by sweaty, grimy-faced little boys who had been paid a penny to make sure the flesh didn't char and to baste the succulent meat with herbs drenched in oil. Indeed, Maldon was full of the mouth-watering smell of roasting meat. The townspeople had put on their best raiment and, even though it was a work day tomorrow, ale and beer were being freely drunk and in the evening the wild dancing would begin. Beatrice, however, had decided to ignore all this. She had left her uncle and aunt, the owners of the Golden Tabard tavern which stood on the outskirts of Maldon, and gone up the dusty trackway to Ravenscroft. For Beatrice this was a splendid day; the sky seemed bluer, the grass greener, the bluebells more magnificent and the air rich with the sweet smells of early summer.

Beatrice had raided the oak chests, taken flour and baked bread and pastries which were now in her wicker basket protected from the flies and heat by a damp linen cloth. Today she would have her own celebration. The Constable of the castle, Sir John Grasse, his wife Anne, Father Aylred the chaplain and Theobald Vavasour the physician were to join her and her beloved, the clerk Ralph Mortimer, for a meal on the castle green. Ralph's boon companion Adam and his wife Marisa had also been invited.

Beatrice tossed back her long, dark hair – 'black as the night' was how Ralph described it. Really she should wear a wimple or veil; Catherine, her aunt, was always lecturing her to do so but Beatrice defied her. Ralph wrote poems about her hair, and about her white skin and sea-grey eyes. Beatrice was in love. Ralph was dearer to her than life itself. Others wondered why, especially the bully-boys and swaggerers who thronged the taproom of the Golden Tabard. They would eye Ralph from head to toe and mutter under their breath about dusty, bare-arsed clerks but Ralph didn't mind. He was sweet-tempered in looks, sweet-tempered by nature; he had close-cropped, dark hair and rather short-sighted, green eyes. Beatrice had met him at a May Fair two years ago. Aunt Catherine and Uncle Robert, her official guardians since she was a child, had disapproved at first but Ralph had charmed them. He was courtly in his ways, always paying for whatever he ate and, now and again, bringing them small gifts – a beeswax candle or a jar of honey from the castle beehives.

Beatrice suddenly started. She'd reached the castle draw-bridge without even noticing it. The guard on duty was sleeping in the shadows, helmet off, spear resting against the wall. And why shouldn't he? True, the peasants in the shires had been threatening revolt and sedition but this was May Day and Sir John Grasse, an old soldier, was a kindly man, no real stickler for discipline. He knew when to bark and when to hold his peace. The Constable preferred to leave all military matters to Beardsmore, his burly sergeant-at-arms. And yet where was he? Still grieving for poor Phoebe? Who had murdered that unfortunate young woman?

Beatrice put such dark thoughts away and clattered across the drawbridge, her pattens beating a rhythm on its wooden boards. She went through the darkened gatehouse and up the winding path which led to the green before the great keep. Above her, the ravens which gave the castle its name swooped and dived against the blue sky. Somewhere on the grass near the moat a pheasant shrieked; finches, who'd built their nests in the walls, warbled and squabbled, filling the late morning with their chatter. A packman passed her, his sumpter pony laden with goods, probably a traveller who had paid to sleep in the castle and would no doubt visit the fair before taking the dusty road north to other Essex towns.

Beatrice turned a corner and paused. The others were already gathered on the green. Lady Anne had laid out a blue broadcloth, with cushions and bolsters arranged as seats. A trestle table had been set up, pewter jugs and cups glinted in the sunlight. Traunchers and platters of bread, cold meat and sliced fruit were covered by white cloths against the marauding flies, attracted by the mounds of manure and ordure piled against the castle walls. Beatrice wrinkled her nose. The smell was not so sweet now. The moat was dank, its water brackish; as Ralph said, you could often smell Ravenscroft before you saw it.

Beatrice hid in the shadows and stared across. These were all her friends: Sir John Grasse, red, jowly face, clean-shaven, his white hair thinning, popping blue eyes and thick, sensuous lips. He had fought with the Black Prince's retinue in France. His wife Anne sat beside him, one arm resting on the back of his chair. She was dressed in a honey-coloured smock, a rather ridiculous, over-blown white wimple around her greying hair. A sharp-featured, keen-eyed woman, slightly younger than her husband, Lady Anne could be a martinet; the garrison was more frightened of her than they were of Sir John. Beside her was Father Aylred in his brown Franciscan robe, head bald as a pigeon's egg – but, as he confessed, he made up for that with a luxurious black beard which fell down to his chest. He was a kindly man and a good priest. Next, Theobald Vavasour, leech and physician, whose grey matted hair reached to below his ears, framing a dusty, tired face. Whatever the weather, Theobald always complained of the cold; even now he wore his patched red cloak lined with ermine, of which he was so proud. He was a true scholar and even possessed a set of eye-glasses so he could examine his patients more closely. He was kindly enough; he distilled perfumes for her from wild flowers. Marisa, her friend, was always borrowing them. She and Adam had also arrived and sat with their backs to her. Adam was blond-haired, tall, thin as a beanpole with light-blue eyes, sharp-faced but ever ready to smile or burst into laughter. His wife Marisa, the Mouse as he nicknamed her, was dressed in her usual grey, her auburn hair carefully hidden by a white starched coif. Ralph always maintained that Marisa reminded him of a nun rather than a young woman in love.

The wine pitcher was being passed round and Sir John had obviously already drunk deeply. Ralph came out on to the steps leading from the keep. Instinctively he stared across.

'Beatrice!' he called. 'Don't hide in the shadows like a ghost!'

She lifted the hem of her sarcenet gown and hastened across the grass. Everyone rose to greet her. Lady Anne, who had always had a special liking for her, grasped her by the shoulders and kissed her on each cheek. Sir John lifted his cup.

'Nothing like a beautiful woman,' he bellowed, 'on a beautiful May Day!'

Theobald winked, Father Aylred sketched a blessing in her direction. Ralph, his fingers and face smudged with ink, linked his arm through hers, plucked the basket from her fingers and placed it on the table.

'I thought you were never coming,' he whispered.

'I had to help in the tavern,' Beatrice hissed back. 'Aunt Catherine is very busy.'

They all sat on cushions, Beatrice next to Adam. Marisa leaned across, her pretty face wreathed in smiles.

'Your last May Day as a maid,' she murmured, smiling at the play of words.

Beatrice blushed. On midsummer's day, 24 June, she and Ralph would exchange vows at the chapel door and be blessed by Father Aylred. Sir John had already declared he would provide a special chamber in Midnight Tower, laughing off Father Aylred's stories that it was haunted. 'They'll be too busy to care!' he roared, not sparing anyone's blushes, including those of his wife. 'A feather mattress, a large four-poster bed, a jug of rich claret and two cups. What more would two lovers need?'

Sir John raised his hand and bellowed at the servants

waiting in the shadow of the wall, 'Come on, you lazy varlets! Let's eat, drink and bless this merry May Day!'

'You've drunk enough for all of us,' Lady Anne snapped.

Sir John just made a rude sound with his lips. The servants filled platters with bread, pastries, chicken legs, succulent sausages, a small portion of shallots, white bread, a dab of butter and took them to each of the diners, with a napkin and small bowl of water in which to wash their fingers. Wine, ale and beer were poured.

It was not yet noon so Beatrice drank only sweet milk, promising Sir John that she would drink when she was ready. Father Aylred said the blessing, they all chanted the 'Ave Maria' in honour of the Blessed Virgin and the meal began. Beatrice found she was hungry and, between mouthfuls, told Marisa the gossip from the taproom. Ralph seemed lost in thought.

'Have you been working?' Beatrice asked him.

'Of course he has,' Adam laughed.

'But not on castle business.' Sir John waved an admonitory finger. 'He's after Brythnoth's treasure.'

'Brythnoth's treasure!' Father Aylred exclaimed.

'Oh, Ralph, you're not still pursuing that?' Adam scoffed.

'Tell us about it,' said Father Aylred. 'I've heard the story before but, like a song, only in snatches.'

Ralph would have refused but Lady Anne insisted. 'Come on, Ralph.'

'It's only a fable.' Ralph pinched Beatrice quickly on the thigh. 'But, centuries ago the pagan Danes landed a raiding

17

force at the mouth of Blackwater River. Brythnoth was a great earl, he marched an army down to meet them. The battle was a fierce one. In fact, there's a poem written about it, copied by the chroniclers. Anyway, Brythnoth refused to leave the field, and he and his men died where they stood. On a silver chain round his neck Brythnoth wore a beautiful jewelled cross. It was made out of pure gold, and it was studded with a costly diamond. Brythnoth knew he was going to die. As his men locked their shields for the final charge, he took the cross off and gave it to one of his squires. Now this young man, whose name was Cerdic, was to take the cross to Brythnoth's wife. He left the battlefield and hurried inland.'

'But he stopped here?' asked Sir John.

'Yes, Sir John, Cerdic stopped here.'

'But Ravenscroft wasn't built then,' Lady Anne declared.

'No, it wasn't,' Ralph agreed, 'but Brythnoth had built a stockade in which he and his men had camped the night before the battle. Cerdic was troubled. Here he was, leaving the battlefield where his master was about to die. People might say that he had taken the cross and played the traitor to Brythnoth. So he buried it, somewhere in the grounds of this castle, and hurried back to the battlefield. When Brythnoth saw him he became enraged. "You have disobeyed my command!" he thundered. "But blood will out and the ravens will feast! I shall die here and so shall ye but your spirit will guard that cross until it is hallowed again."'

'What does that mean?' Marisa asked.

'Until the cross is found,' Ralph explained, 'and re-blessed.'

Father Aylred looked solemn. 'And Brythnoth and Cerdic died?'

'Oh yes, back to back in the press of the fight. They say the Blackwater ran with blood for days afterwards.'

'And the cross?' Theobald asked eagerly.

Ralph shrugged. 'No one knows. Except . . .' he paused for effect, 'after the battle the Danes, who knew about this great treasure, searched for Brythnoth's corpse. They found him lying beneath Cerdic. The young squire was still alive and the Danish chief demanded to know where the cross was. Cerdic smiled. "On an altar to your God and mine." That's all he said before he, too, died.'

'What did he mean?' Father Aylred asked.

Ralph laughed. 'If I knew that, Father, I'd find the treasure.'

'So you look among the manuscripts for clues,' said Father Aylred.

'The tale appears in many forms, handed down from one chronicler to another,' Ralph explained. 'It is recorded that even those who built this castle searched for the cross. The legends have multiplied.' He glanced sideways at Beatrice. 'One, which first appeared in the reign of the King's great-grandfather, says that only lovers will find Brythnoth's cross.'

'In which case you are well qualified,' Father Aylred laughed. 'Ralph, Beatrice, I look forward to your wedding day.' A cloud crossed the sun and the Franciscan shivered. 'I wonder if Cerdic can hear us now?'

'Quite possibly,' said Lady Anne. 'According to local lore, this castle is truly haunted.'

'Is it?' Marisa asked excitedly.

'Yes, and not only by Cerdic,' declared Adam, eager to show his knowledge. He sipped from his pewter cup. 'There are other ghosts here as well.'

'Oh, go on, tell us,' Beatrice urged, though she noticed how troubled Father Aylred had become.

'Ravenscroft was first built during a time of terror and devastation in Essex,' Adam recounted. 'The castle was owned by a robber baron, Sir Geoffrey de Mandeville, a true spawn of Satan, a fiend in human flesh. Sir Geoffrey ravaged to his heart's content. He brought back prisoners to be tortured by his master executioner, a man called Black Malkyn. Malkyn liked nothing better than to see his prisoners suffer excruciating pain. He used the thumb screw, the rack, the pulley, the bed of nails.' Adam lowered his voice. 'Sometimes he would fill the dungeons with flesh-eating rats.'

'Oh, stop it!' Marisa cried.

'But it's true,' Sir John said. 'Sir Geoffrey was a devil incarnate. He built our Midnight Tower.' He pointed across to the great ragstone tower built into the curtain wall.

'I must admit,' declared Father Aylred, 'I do not like the place, it's cold and dank.' He lowered his head and mumbled something.

Beatrice was sure she heard the word exorcise.

'Oh, it's cheery enough,' Sir John scoffed. 'You just have a fanciful imagination, Father. Anyway, Sir Geoffrey used to go out raiding,' he winked at his wife, 'searching for soft virginal flesh to satisfy his lusts, gold and silver to fill his treasury.'

'I'd take your ears if you did that!' Lady Anne retorted.

Sir John patted his wife affectionately on the knee. 'Sir Geoffrey had a wife, the Lady Johanna, a beautiful young woman. A ray of light in the gathering darkness around Mandeville. She was repelled by her husband, so the legends say. Isn't that right, Ralph?'

The clerk nodded.

'Lady Johanna fell in love with a young squire. When Sir Geoffrey was away, they'd meet in her chamber in the Midnight Tower.' Sir John glanced at Father Aylred. 'Well, just to console themselves. One day Sir Geoffrey came back and surprised the lovers. Lady Johanna was immured for life in a dungeon beneath the tower. The young squire was handed over to Black Malkyn. For days that limb of Hell tortured the young man in a room next to Lady Johanna's cell. She had to sit and listen to his shrieks and screams.' Sir John sat back and drank his wine.

'Oh, finish the story!' said Lady Anne impatiently.

Sir John needed no more encouragement. 'Well, one night the screams ceased,' he said ominously. 'Lady Johanna, who had been left for days without water or food, was now given some meat and a cup of wine. The dish was pushed through a small slit in the wall. She had to eat it, drink the wine and hand it back. This went on for months. The food and wine

21

were always delivered when the bells of the castle sounded midnight.'

'Oh, I think I know what you're going to say.' Marisa put her fingers to her mouth and drew closer to Adam.

'One night the meat and wine stopped being served. Lady Johanna looked through the narrow slit in her cell. She pleaded with her husband to set her free. "Oh no," that evil man replied. "Tonight at midnight I will brick up this wall totally. There will be no more food or wine."'

'Be careful how you tell this part,' Lady Anne warned.

'Well, Lady Johanna asked why, so that scion of Satan told her the truth. The meat she had eaten was the salted flesh of her lover whom Black Malkyn had torn to pieces, and the wine cup she had been using was fashioned from the skull of her dead lover.'

'Oh, no!' Beatrice exclaimed. 'Sir John, that is a hideous story!'

Sir John drank from his cup and smacked his lips. 'Well, that's why they call it the Midnight Tower. On the anniversary of Lady Johanna's death, you can hear her dying screams and cries of horror as her brain turned mad before her body failed her.'

'Is the cell still there?' Marisa asked.

'It could be.' Sir John's eyes widened. 'There are store-rooms in that part now, passageways and galleries. No one has ever looked, so no one knows what might be hidden there.'

'That's enough,' Lady Anne declared. 'You'll frighten us all. This is May Day!'

The conversation turned to other events. Father Aylred expressed his concern at the discontent in Maldon and the outlying villages where the peasants fumed and seethed with anger at the impositions laid on them by the great lords who held their wages down and kept them shackled to the soil. 'They are only poor earthworms,' Father Aylred said. 'And similar discontent is apparently spreading like fire among the stubble in other shires. There is talk of a great revolt, of a peasant army, more than the leaves in autumn, gathering and marching on London.'

'If that happens,' said Sir John stoutly, tapping the hilt of his dagger, 'Ravenscroft will drop its portcullis and raise the drawbridge.' He glanced round. 'We are all the King's men here. If the black banner of rebellion is unfurled, we will do our best to defend the King's rights.'

'But they are poor men and women,' Father Aylred protested. 'Their children grow thin, their bellies sag with hunger.'

'I know, I know.' Sir John was a kindly man and Beatrice could see he was deeply worried. 'I've done the best I can. I've given grain from the storerooms and I've warned the tax collector not to shear their sheep so close.'

'Well, thank God that person's not at our feast!' Lady Anne snapped.

They all murmured in agreement. A week earlier Goodman Winthrop, a tax collector from London, had arrived at the castle: a lanky, balding, snivel-nosed individual dressed in a grey fustian robe and high-heeled leather riding boots.

Goodman Winthrop was a lawyer sent by the Exchequer to collect the poll tax in Ravenscroft, Maldon and the outlying areas. A sour, dour man who seemed to take delight in the task assigned to him, he had arrived accompanied by a clerk and four royal archers. He had demanded the protection of Ravenscroft Castle; Sir John had reluctantly agreed, on one condition, that Goodman Winthrop should not begin his tax collecting until after May Day. Sir John had provided him and his escort with chambers near the barbican overlooking the moat. 'Maybe the smell will drive him out,' he commented. 'A more miserable caitiff I've never met.'

Fortunately, Goodman had kept to himself.

'He had the cheek to try and invite himself to our celebrations,' Sir John growled now. 'I told him to go and join those on the green. I am sure the good people of Maldon will give him a welcome he'll never forget!'

'He's also very interested in the legend,' Adam remarked. 'Last Sunday, just after we had gathered for vespers in the chapel, he took me aside. Full of the stories about Brythnoth's cross, he was. I told you about it, Ralph. He had even searched among the manuscripts at the Inns of Court for references to it.'

Ralph, his face flushed with wine, snorted with laughter and tapped the side of his nose. 'Goodman Winthrop should be busy about his taxes. I'm much nearer the treasure than anyone will ever be.'

Lady Anne leaned across. 'Ralph, do you really think you could find it?'

Ralph was embarrassed. 'I'm just playing with words,' he stammered. 'Master Winthrop's long nose could be used for better purposes,' he continued quickly, eager to divert attention. 'I mean the murder of poor Phoebe.'

His words created an immediate silence.

'Poor Phoebe,' Father Aylred echoed.

Sir John pursed his lips and nodded solemnly. 'A terrible murder. The guard who found her corpse is still being sick, says he cannot forget. Beardsmore's taken up with rage and sorrow.'

Everyone sat in silence. Three days earlier Phoebe, a maid from the castle, a buxom, bright-eyed lass, had left to return to her parents in their wattle-daubed cottage on the main trackway out of Maldon. When she did not arrive home, her father came to the castle the following morning to look for her. Beardsmore, the sergeant-at-arms, had taken charge; he was beside himself with worry. He had been on guard the previous night and had not seen Phoebe leave. He was sure his sweetheart was still in the castle. Still, a search had been organised and, within the hour, Phoebe's body had been found in Devil's Spinney, a copse of ancient oaks, only a short distance from the castle. Phoebe's throat had been cut from ear to ear and it was apparent, so Theobald Vavasour said, that she had been attacked and cruelly beaten before she was killed.

'Who could do that to a poor girl?' Father Aylred asked.

'I . . .' Beatrice stared across at an old mangonel which lay on its side on the far side of the green.

'Go on, Beatrice,' Ralph urged. 'Tell Sir John.'

'When I left on Monday,' she said, 'I thought I saw someone near Devil's Spinney. All I glimpsed was a cowl and cloak, it could have been anyone.'

'The roads are full of wolf's-heads and outlaws,' Sir John commented. 'Landless men who prey upon the weak.'

Ralph shook his head. 'The trackway from the castle is fairly busy. Whoever killed Phoebe would have had to lure her into the spinney first, and no stranger could have done that.'

'You're saying that Phoebe must have gone to the spinney of her own free will to meet someone – the person Beatrice saw – who later killed her?'

'Perhaps,' Ralph replied.

'It's all very unsettling.' Father Aylred was pale-faced and anxious. 'Phoebe's murder, Beardsmore vowing vengeance and that cesspool of discontent, the Pot of Thyme.' He was referring to a tavern in Maldon, a well-known meeting place for malcontents.

'It's seething over the disappearance of Fulk the miller's son.'

'What happened to him?'

'No one knows. They say he came to Ravenscroft and hasn't been seen since.'

'Oh, enough of all this.' Lady Anne got to her feet. 'Tax collectors, witches, ghosts, murders! Now, I've made something special.'

'Oh good!' Ralph rubbed his stomach; Lady Anne's spiced cheese dish was famous.

'And for afterwards,' she said, 'some oriels. You all like elderberry, don't you?'

They all did and Sir John, eager to keep everyone happy, said he would serve some of his Rhenish wine which was kept cool in the castle cellars.

Adam brought out his flute and Ralph sang a song to the Virgin Mary, 'Maria Dulcis Mater', in a lusty voice, a fine complement to Adam's playing. The afternoon drew on. Each of the guests had to sing a song or recite a poem. The sun began to set. Wheeled braziers were lit and brought out, and pitch torches fired and lashed to poles driven into the ground. Their flames spluttered and danced in the night air.

'We shall feast and we shall feast,' Sir John declared, 'until we have feasted enough. Then Lady Anne here will serve some marchpane.'

'Time for a pause, I think,' said Theobald. 'A brisk walk, clear the dishes and the tables, then some marchpane. Afterwards we can sit here and really frighten ourselves with ghost stories.'

'Come on.' Lady Anne beckoned to Marisa and Beatrice. 'Help me carry these pots to the kitchens. The scullery maids can wash them.'

Ralph pinched the back of Beatrice's hand. 'I'll go for a walk along the parapet.' He pointed to the deserted sentry walk high on the wall. 'The night air is always invigorating.'

Beatrice and Marisa helped Lady Anne to collect the cups, empty bowls and jugs and take them into the chamber at the base of the keep. Scullions had prepared small vats full of hot water so the dishes could be soaked and washed. Beatrice chatted to Marisa for a while and then went back to the green. It was deserted now. The guests had dispersed to the latrines, or to wash or simply to walk off the effects of their feasting. Beatrice stood and stared at the large blue cloth, the great torches on either side, their flames casting strange shadows. She repressed a chill of fear. No more celebrations now. No merriment. It looked a ghostly place. She glanced across at Midnight Tower and wondered what horrors lurked there. She noticed that the parapet walk was dark; the torch which should have been lashed there must have fallen and gone out.

'I'll go up,' she decided. 'It will be nice to walk with Ralph and take the cool of the night.'

She hurried up the steps. At the top the wind whipped her hair. She stared out over the moat towards Devil's Spinney where the great oak trees loomed like petrified monsters against the night sky. What secrets did they hold? she wondered. Why had little Phoebe gone there? She peered ahead of her. Ralph should be here. She hurried along, remembering not to look to her left or right. Ralph had taught her that. 'Never look down and you'll never be dizzy,' he had advised. The door to Midnight Tower was open. She glimpsed a shape then something hit the ground in front of her, ringing like a fairy bell.

Was someone throwing coins at her? Beatrice bent down to pick it up. She heard a sound, a footstep and, as she raised her head, a terrible blow to her temples sent her flying through the night air to crash on to the cobbles below.

Chapter 2

Beatrice stared down. She'd felt such terrible pains, as if her body was caught and licked by raging fire, but something was wrong. Was she dreaming? She was wearing the same kirtle. She touched her head. There was no pain now. Her hair still hung unbound, cork pattens on her feet, yet there was a body lying on the cobbles before her: eyes open, a line of blood trickling out between parted lips, head twisted strangely, arms out, fingers splayed. It was herself!

I must be dreaming, in a faint or a swoon, Beatrice thought. She heard a voice call, the sound of footsteps. People came running up: Theobald Vavasour, Father Aylred, Adam and Marisa. All gathered, crouching round her body.

'No, I'm all right!' she called out.

Her friends did not respond, yet she was sure she had spoken, she'd heard her own words and she could still feel the cold night air, although the light had changed to a strange bronze colour and it was eerie.

Ralph appeared, running down the steps. He stood on the

cobbles and stared across at the small group, his mouth opening and closing.

'Beatrice!' he yelled. 'Beatrice!'

She ran across to meet him but she couldn't touch him. He seemed to run through her. Sir John came out of the tower, followed by Lady Anne. Beatrice tried to clutch them but it was like trying to seize the air. She went to stand with them. Ralph was leaning over her body, shaking his head. He tried to clutch her but Father Aylred gently blocked him.

'She's dead, Ralph. God save her, she's dead. There's nothing we can do.'

Theobald had his hand pressed against her neck then felt her wrist, searching for the blood pulse. Beatrice was filled with horror.

'I am not dead!' she called. 'I'm here!'

Her words echoed strangely across the bailey.

'I'm not dead!' she cried. 'I'm here! I love Ralph! We are going to be married!'

'She must have fallen,' Adam said. 'She probably went up to the parapet walk to look for Ralph.'

Ralph had his face in his hands. 'I went to my chamber,' he murmured. 'I had a May Day present for her.' He took his hands away, fumbled in his pouch and brought out a small brooch carved in the shape of a griffin. It was silver and studded with tiny glass stones.

'Oh, but it's beautiful,' Beatrice murmured. She stretched out her hand but her fingers couldn't clutch the brooch. I was like a dream in which she watched herself walk, talk, eat and drink.

'She must have stumbled on the parapet,' Sir John said. 'Poor child, no one could survive such a fall. Theobald, Father Aylred, Adam, let's take her up to the chapel. You,' he gestured at Beardsmore who stood a short way off, 'did you see anything untoward?'

'No, sir. We heard a cry and saw something fall, a blur against the night.'

'We'll let her lie before the altar in the chapel,' Father Aylred agreed.

'I'll dress the corpse for burial,' Lady Anne offered. 'I'll wash her poor body, dress her in one of my gowns.'

'It's summer.' Father Aylred patted Ralph on the shoulder. 'I'll sing the Requiem Mass tomorrow. We have no choice, Ralph. She must be buried as soon as possible.'

Ralph wasn't listening, he was in shock, his face pallid, his mouth open, a drool of saliva running down his chin. Marisa came and put her arm round his waist.

'Come,' she said. 'Come to the kitchens, I'll give you some mulled wine.'

'I want to . . .'

'No, it's best if you don't, Ralph.' Father Aylred was firm.

Beatrice could stand this no longer. She was dreaming! Yet how could she be? She could see them. When she wanted she could smell the midden, look up at the sky, feel the breeze, but it was as if she was divided from them by a wall of thick but lucidly clear glass. Whatever she did, whatever she said made no impact.

They were gently picking up her body on a makeshift bier, a cloth slung between two poles. Now she looked as if she was sleeping. Someone had closed her eyes. Beatrice gave a loud scream and sank to the cobbles. All she could think of was Ralph. All she wanted was to hold his hand and tell him how much she loved him, how she wanted to be his wife and they would live for ever. Now that was all gone. They were walking away as if she was no more.

'Oh Jesus miserere!' she whispered. 'Oh, Lord Jesus, Holy Mary! How can I be dead?' The souls of the departed, weren't they whisked off to Heaven, Hell or Purgatory? Isn't that what Father Aylred had preached? Yet nothing had changed. She was in life but not of it.

Beatrice got to her feet and breathed in. She laughed. If she was dead why did she need air? I want to be warm, she thought, and became aware of heat, as if she was standing before the roaring fire in the taproom of the Golden Tabard. Uncle Robert and Aunt Catherine! I must tell them.

Beatrice ran across the cobbles but her feet made no sound. She found she could move, as in a dream, and not stop for rest. A man on horseback rode out of the stables. She halted, terrified the horse was going to crash into her, but both horse and rider passed on. She felt nothing. Beatrice looked over her shoulder and again became aware of that strange bronze light as if everything was tainted with a copper tinge. The green had changed. A gallows stood where the blue cloth

32

had been spread for their feast earlier in the day; from the rope hung a decomposing cadaver, neck awry, hands tied behind its back. Beatrice screamed. A knight came galloping across the cobbles. A terrible vision of armour and horseflesh. Beneath the conical nose guard, Beatrice glimpsed cruel eyes, a drooping moustache, twisted mouth. He wore chain mail and leggings, not like any knight or soldier Beatrice had ever seen. Other changes were taking place. Spheres of golden light moved backwards and forwards, silver discs sparkled, circling the castle bailey like bubbles sprung from warm soapy water. There was a table she hadn't seen before. On it lay a white skeleton, its bones picked clean, the skull hanging awry. Dark shapes scurried around.

Beatrice felt frightened. If she was dead then the Lord Jesus would help her. The castle yard was the same yet it wasn't. Shadows were moving in and out of doorways. She moved towards the steps of the keep then paused. A young man was walking towards her. Despite the night she could make out his features: round-faced, smooth-shaven, merry mouth and laughing eyes. He was dressed in an old-fashioned cote-hardie which fell to his knees, a war belt strapped round his waist. His hair was oily and combed back. He walked with a swagger, and as he passed he smiled and winked.

'Be careful!' he whispered then strode on.

Beatrice whirled round. The figure disappeared in the gathering darkness. So, she thought, some people can see me. She stared up at the parapet.

33

'I didn't fall,' she murmured. She touched the side of her head. 'I was struck.'

She jumped as a great mastiff, with fiery eyes and slavering jaws, came bounding up to her. She stood transfixed in terror as the beast leapt, only to pass through her, racing into the night. She hurried up towards the door of the keep, moving so fast she didn't realise until it had happened that she had gone through the door without opening it. She was standing at the foot of the spiral staircase leading up to the chapel.

Beatrice closed her eyes. 'I really am dead,' she murmured.

She opened her mouth and gave the most hideous, heart-rending scream. She waited. Those in the chapel above must have heard her. Someone would come running down the steps. But they didn't. Again she screamed like a soul in mortal agony.

'Who are you?'

Beatrice whirled round. She gazed in dread at the gargoyle figure before her. He was tall, well over two yards high, with a bulbous, grotesque face, cheeks pitted and scarred, eyes thin and glittering under a mop of dirty red hair. A broad, leather belt circled his swollen stomach, and from it hung keys and a dagger. The high-heeled boots he wore were spurred.

'I'm dreaming,' she murmured, stepping back.

'Ye not be dreaming!' The man stood, head slightly cocked. 'If ye can see Black Malkyn, then ye not be dreaming! Ye be dead!' His hideous smile disappeared as a dreadful scream pierced the night.

'What was that?' Beatrice demanded.

'That be Lady Johanna.' His face became sad. 'Like you, like me, one of the Incorporeals.'

And he was gone, walking through the wall, spurs clinking, heading towards Midnight Tower. Beatrice climbed the stairs. She could do this effortlessly; there was no need to stop to catch her breath. As she turned a corner, following the spiral staircase up, what looked like a monk in a dirty grey robe passed her. She glimpsed white, pinched features though he seemed unaware of her.

Beatrice entered the chapel. Her corpse now lay in a casket just within the door of the rood screen. Father Aylred was kneeling in prayers. There was no sign of the others. Beatrice approached her corpse. In the light of the flickering candles, the face looked pallid, the horrid gash vivid in the side of her head. Beatrice glanced up at the pyx which held the Blessed Sacrament. Surely, if she was dead, the good Lord Jesus would help.

She went towards the sanctuary steps, intending to grasp the pyx, but the spheres of light, those circles of fiery light which she'd glimpsed in the courtyard below, sprang up all around her. They came together, forming an impenetrable wall between her and the altar. She pressed against them. She felt warm and happy. She caught a beautiful fragrance like the most costly pefume. A sound of singing, children laughing. She wanted to go through this wall of light but she couldn't. She stared at it and became aware of faces within the spheres of light. Children's faces, small, beautifully formed, hair framing silver cheeks, eyes like sapphires. Again she pressed but the heat became so intense she had to stand back.

'Go no further!' A voice spoke from this wall of gold. 'Go no further till your appointed time!'

Beatrice paused.

'Or, if you wish,' the voice came as a whisper, 'if you really want to, come towards the light.'

Beatrice took a step forward yet found she couldn't go any further. Not because of any hindrance. She thought of Ralph, of her wedding day, of that walk along the lonely parapet and that dreadful blow to her head.

Spinning on her heel, Beatrice fled from the chapel, down the steps and out into the courtyard. She stopped there, agitated, troubled. She screamed, yet she knew in her heart of hearts that no one would hear her, no one could see her. Was this how it would be always? Locked here in this strange world for ever? Something caught her eye, a silver disc of light shimmered then disappeared.

Dark shapes thronged all about her. Thoughts came in rapid succession. She now had no problem with memories. Her mother and father had died when she was young but now she saw them clearly. Her mother's kindly, plump face; her father, who had worked as a weaver, standing in the doorway of some house, a piece of fabric across his arms; the day she had met Ralph; people she had known as a child. It was as if she was alive in both the past and the present. Yet she wasn't alive! She was here clothed in the attire she had put on this morning after she'd washed her hands and face. She could see the hem of her dress, the cuffs, the bracelets on her wrist but no one else could. She closed her eyes. Nothing but darkness! How long would such confusion last?

Beatrice was roused by a rattle of chains. A strange cavalcade was making its way through the gate, that terrible knight she had glimpsed earlier astride a great black warhorse. Its harness and saddle were of silver, edged with scarlet trimming. He was accompanied by a gaggle of riders dressed in animal pelts. They were drinking and cursing. Behind them a group of men, manacled and chained together, straggled across the castle yard which now seemed different. Buildings she was accustomed to had disappeared. The devilish cavalcade stopped. The knight dismounted. He issued orders in a tongue she did not understand. His voice was sharp and guttural. The prisoners were made to kneel and their wooden neck collars were removed. Beatrice watched in horror as the prisoners were forced down. The knight drew a great two-handed sword out of the scabbard hanging from his saddle horn. Beatrice screamed as he lifted the sword and, in one swift cut, decapitated a prisoner. He moved along the line like a gardener pruning flowers. Time and again that dreadful sword rose and fell. Heads bounced on to the cobbles, blood spouting. The cadavers stayed upright and then fell, jerking spasmodically.

'Don't!' Beatrice screamed. 'Oh, for the love of God, don't!'

She ran across, intent on grasping the knight's arm but again she clutched moonbeams. The knight kept cutting and slicing. The yard stank of the iron tang of blood. Beatrice looked up at the night sky.

'What is this?' she screamed. 'I am dead and the living can't see me! I am dead and those who have died can't see me!'

Perhaps it was some dreadful nightmare. She ran up the steps leading to the parapet walk from which she had fallen. She reached the top. A soldier was standing on guard there. His dress was similar to that of the horrid spectre she had seen murdering the prisoners in the bailey below. She reached out but felt nothing. She clutched the crenellated battlements and stared over. The castle wall was bathed in a strange bronze light. Horror piled upon horror! Corpses were hanging in chains from the battlements. She ran along the parapet walk. The door to the tower was open. The young man she had glimpsed before was standing there smiling at her.

'Go carefully!' he warned.

Beatrice ignored him. She stood on the edge of the parapet and stared down. The hideous execution scene had disappeared. The yard was as she'd known it; the blue cloth was still spread over the grass. Adam and Marisa were standing by the keep door. They were joined by Father Aylred. A messenger left, spurring his horse towards the barbican. A wild thought seized Beatrice. She was dreaming and to prove it she would jump from the parapet and before she hit the ground she would wake up in her little cot bed above the taproom in the Golden Tabard. She would cry out. Aunt Catherine would come hurrying in to embrace her and tell her not to worry about horrid night-mares.

Beatrice felt the cold night air on her face. She spread her arms like a bird taking flight and launched herself into the darkness. She reached the cobbles. No pain, no flesh-juddering impact, no taste of blood spilling into her mouth, no last dying moments. It was as if she had taken a small step.

'Beatrice! Beatrice Arrowner!'

She spun round. A young man stood there. He had blond hair, a smooth face, and was dressed exquisitely in a short cote-hardie, lined and trimmed with fur, parti-coloured hose and a rather exaggerated codpiece. On his feet were long pointed shoes, the toes curled back and fastened to garters below his knee. In one hand he carried a chaperon, and a brocaded dagger sheath hung from his silver belt. He was sniffing at a pomander, red in colour and decorated with gold and silver thread.

'Who are you?'

The young man smiled. He was beautiful, like a courtier who had passed through Maldon on his way to Westminster some months ago. That visitor to the Golden Tabard had arrogant eyes and a petulant mouth. This young man was friendly, smiling, the lips open to reveal white, even teeth. He walked closer. She could smell the fragrance of his clothes. He offered her the pomander. She didn't take it but caught a perfume like roses crushed in fresh water.

'Who are you?' she repeated. 'Where am I? Can you

please help me, sir?' A silver disc shimmered on the edge of her vision.

'You are Beatrice Arrowner. You died in a fall from the parapet wall.'

'I know that!' Beatrice snapped. 'But what has happened? I saw a knight dark and hideous. He was here in the yard slaughtering men. A great mastiff hurled itself at me. Look!' She pointed at the dark shapes flitting around her.

'Just phantasms,' the young man replied.

'Who are you?' she insisted.

'Oh, quite petulant, aren't we? Fiery-tempered Beatrice. My name, well, you can call me Crispin.'

'Are you a ghost, Crispin?'

'I am what you see, Beatrice. I am what you want me to be.'

Beatrice felt uneasy. Crispin was standing there like some beautiful Christ statue in church but the night around him seemed darker, denser; the silver disc had disappeared.

'I did not die,' she blurted, suddenly angry. 'I was murdered!'

'I know,' said Crispin smoothly.

'And do you also know who is responsible?'

He shook his head. 'If I did, Beatrice, I'd tell you. So, what do you think of it, Beatrice, eh? Not yet eighteen summers old and snatched out of life. No Ralph, no wedding day, no warm embrace or sweet kisses.'

'Where is Ralph?' Beatrice asked.

Crispin pointed to the Lion Tower. 'He's in his chamber.

He's drunk deeply, Beatrice. He thinks wine will ease the pain, and perhaps it will. In time he will forget you. It could have been so different, couldn't it?'

'Yes!' Her voice came out as a snarl, so sharp, so hate-filled, even she was surprised.

'And what about Uncle Robert and Aunt Catherine? Those poor guardians who regarded you as their only child? Riven with grief, they are.' Crispin sniffed at the pomander. 'What a waste,' he whispered. He glanced mice-eyed at her. 'Do you want vengeance, Beatrice? I can help you.' He stepped a little closer, his light-blue eyes full of kindness, red lips parted.

Impulsively Beatrice stood up on tiptoe and kissed him. She felt strange, on the one hand attracted to this beautiful young man, on the other, troubled by the hate his words stirred up in her.

'I'll give you another thought,' Crispin whispered. 'And listen to me now. Were you the real victim?'

'What do you mean?' she gasped.

'Think about it. Just think.' His words came in a hiss.

'Beatrice! Beatrice Arrowner!'

She whirled round. The merry-faced man she had glimpsed earlier was sitting, cross-legged, on the blue cloth.

'Come away, Beatrice,' he murmured. 'Ralph is crying.'

'Oh, ignore him!' Crispin retorted. 'He's a liar and a thief!'

Beatrice stepped back. She was being so selfish. Ralph was crying. She should comfort him. As she moved away, Crispin's eyes turned hard.

'I'll come back,' she whispered. 'I promise. I must see Ralph.'

'Of course, Beatrice,' he said and turned away.

Beatrice was already in the tower hurrying up the spiral staircase, aware of the torches, the dancing shadows, of grotesque shapes, odious smells and macabre forms. She reached Ralph's room and passed through the door into the small, circular chamber. Beatrice gave a deep sigh of grief. The room was so familiar, so full of loving memories: the rushes on the floor, green and supple; the little pots of herbs she had brought; the crucifix on the wall; the small triptych on the table next to the bed.

Ralph was sprawled there. In the light of the capped candle she could see he was asleep but his cheeks were tear-stained. He moved and jerked, muttering to himself. On the floor lay a cup in a puddle of spilled wine. Beatrice was filled with a deep longing. She wanted to stretch out and touch him but she could feel nothing. She lay down on the bed next to him as if she was his handfast wife. She put her arm round him and kissed him on the cheek, whispering his name. She told him how she loved him and would do so for all eternity. Ralph stirred and moved. He called out her name, his eyes opened and closed. He groaned and dug his face deep into the bolster. Beatrice stroked his hair and tried to dry the tears on his cheeks.

'Oh Ralph, Ralph!' she whispered. 'Oh sweetheart!'

He moved and turned. Beatrice felt as if she was crying herself.

'It's all invisible,' she murmured. 'My tears mean nothing.'

She recalled Crispin's words and the flame of anger and hatred seethed. What did he mean, was she the real victim? She sat up and stared across at the crucifix and noticed a silver disc of light was moving around it. She glanced away. Everything had been a mockery. Where was Heaven? Where was the good Lord Jesus? The angels, all the mysteries the Church had taught? She had been cast up like a rotten boat on the banks of a sluggish river. All she could do was watch the water run by. How long would this go on? For ever? Sealed in this existence for all eternity? She kissed Ralph on the brow and walked out of the chamber.

'Well, Beatrice?' Crispin was standing in the stairwell. 'All gone,' he said. 'Lost like tears in the rain. Come.'

He took her by the hand and she didn't resist. They walked out to Midnight Tower and up flights of steps. Beatrice found herself in Adam's room. He and Marisa were lying, fully clothed, on the bed, arms about each other. Marisa was crying. Adam was soothing her, stroking her hair.

'So unnecessary,' Crispin's voice murmured.

Beatrice felt a surge of resentment. She and Ralph should be lying like this. Why her? Why now? And before Crispin could say another word, she turned and fled down the stairs. Crispin called after her but Beatrice didn't care. She crashed into the wall and slipped but felt no pain. She stopped and laughed hysterically. A silver disc hovered above her. She drove it away with her hand as a child would a ball. She reached the bottom of the tower and stopped. A woman blocked her way. Tall, hair as black as a raven's wing, her face could have been beautiful but it was white and ghastly with red-rimmed, staring eyes. Her lovely samite dress was dirt-stained. She stared malevolently at Beatrice and, opening her mouth, screamed like a wild animal. Beatrice stood her ground. The woman advanced. Beatrice recoiled at the disgusting smell which emanated from her.

'Who are you?'

'Welcome to the kingdom of the dead, Beatrice Arrowner. Look at me and weep. Lady Johanna de Mandeville, walled up, tombed in for death. Nothing but darkness. He shouldn't have done it. It was cruel and no one raised a hand. No pity in life, no mercy in death. Nothing but a desert of hate and chambers full of spectres!'

Beatrice could stand no more and fled like a shadow from Midnight Tower.

Chapter 3

Beatrice found herself on the path leading from the barbican. The stars were bright above her, the silver moon slipped in and out of the clouds yet it wasn't the usual blue-black of country nights. The heathland, Devil's Spinney and the walls of Ravenscroft were bathed in that eerie bronze tinge, like light reflected in a brass pot. The silence, too, was strange, not the calm and peace of the countryside at night but more threatening, as if other phantasms lurked behind the curtain of night, ready to spring out. Beatrice stopped and looked back at the castle. She'd walked this way earlier, her mind full of Ralph, May celebrations and, of course, her wedding day. The castle had always seemed friendly with its familiar turrets and towers. Now it looked foreign. Where there had been windows were now plain bricks, strange emblems and pennants flew from the ramparts, and ghostly lights glowed on the tops of the towers.

A group of horsemen burst out of Devil's Spinney, fleeing like bats under the moon. They charged towards the drawbridge,

thundering across in ghostly cavalcade – a vision of things as
they once were rather than the reality she had left. Strange
cries overhead made Beatrice glance up at the sky and she
saw geese-like forms flying between the clouds. Fires burnt
in Devil's Spinney and loud shouts and cries came from
the darkness on her right. Beatrice felt afraid and then
laughed.

'If I am dreaming,' she murmured, 'then I shall wake up and
these are nothing but phantasms. If I am truly dead, separated
from Ralph, then what else can happen to me?'

She walked on and came to the crossroads. She recognised
them immediately but not the gibbet which stretched out
against the night sky or the grisly cadaver which hung in
chains from its rusting hook. Beneath it a young woman,
red hair falling down to her shoulders and dressed in a white
shift, was staring in horror at the great bloody patch on her
chest. She raised her head as Beatrice approached.

'Who are you?' the young woman asked. Her face was
ghoulish, her eyes like those of a dead fish, the pallid skin
of her hands tinged with dirt and mud.

'I am Beatrice Arrowner.'

'And I am Etheldreda.' She saw the puzzlement in Beatrice's
face. 'We see each other, we can talk and hear.' Etheldreda
smiled in a show of blackened teeth. 'But we are of the nether
world, in the kingdom of the dead.'

'Why don't you leave?' Beatrice asked. As soon as the
words were out, she realised this was how she used to speak
in dreams.

46

'I cannot leave,' Etheldreda moaned. 'So long ago yet just like yesterday. What year is it?'

Beatrice stared at her. 'I am not too sure.'

'Well, who is King?'

'Young Richard reigns in Westminster.' Beatrice recalled the proclamations read out in the parish church four years ago after the old King had died. 'It is the year of Our Lord 1381.'

'Young Richard?' Etheldreda stared at her, lips opening and closing like a landed carp. 'Has time passed so quickly? In the parish church Father Bernard preached against King John.'

'King John? But he lived many years ago. The ancient ones tell stories about him. How he marched through Wessex and lost his treasure in the Wash.'

'Where's that?' Etheldreda asked.

'To the north,' Beatrice replied. 'Where the sea comes in and drowns the fields.'

Etheldreda nodded her head. 'Aye,' she murmured. 'And I drowned myself in Blackwater. Seduced, I was, by Simon the reeve.' Her dead eyes filled with tears. 'Promised we'd become handfast, he did. On Midsummer Day, yes, that's it, we were drinking midsummer ales. He spurned me, laughed with the other men. I fled the fair and went down to Blackwater. All I remember is jumping, the water filling my mouth and nose. Even as it did, I didn't want to die. Yet they took my corpse, drove a stake through my heart and buried me here at the crossroads.'

'Why don't you move?' Beatrice asked kindly. 'Come
She held out her hand.

Etheldreda turned away. 'I cannot,' she answered wearil
'I will not. If I stay here they might come back. If I wait lo
enough, Simon the reeve will walk this way. I will speak
him about his unkindly words.'

Beatrice shook her head. 'But that is all gone.'

Etheldreda looked away, staring into the darkness witho
speaking.

Beatrice walked on. She reached the village church of
Dunstan's and paused outside the lych gate, gazing acro
the cemetery. She had played here as a child. Now it w
full of forms and shapes. Piteous cries rang out like those
wild geese in autumn. Beatrice hurried on, fearful of bei
caught by the likes of Etheldreda.

She reached the high street, pleased to be in famili
surroundings. There was Thurston the weaver's house, Walt
the brewer's and the Pot of Thyme, an alehouse of ill repu
despite its name. Its shutters were thrown open, lights, so
and chatter broke the darkness. Beatrice paused. She w
unsure if she was seeing things as they were or other visio
of the night. The door opened and Goodman Winthr
lurched out, swaying on his feet, one arm round a tave
wench, the other pushing down her dirty, low-cut bodic
fondling her breasts as he tried to kiss her. The wen
shrieked with laughter and led him on. Goodman Winthrop
belly was full of ale. If it hadn't been for his companio
he would have fallen flat on his face. Beatrice watch

them go up the street. The man was a fool. He was a tax collector yet he'd come unguarded into the village to sup among his enemies. Did he think that on May Day memories faded? Alarmed, Beatrice followed the swaying couple. Now and again they'd stop so Goodman Winthrop could steady himself.

'Be careful, sir!' Beatrice called.

The darkness around Goodman Winthrop was deeper than the night. She ran up behind him. Goodman was whispering obscenities into the wench's ear, trying to persuade her to return with him to the castle. She was acting the reluctant maid. Beatrice felt both sad and responsible. Goodman Winthrop should have been invited to their feast. After all, he was a guest at Ravenscroft. He must have witnessed their celebrations as well as those in the town and become morose, letting wine and ill judgement get the better of his wit. They stopped beneath an apothecary's sign.

'Come back with me,' Winthrop slurred.

The young woman giggled.

'I have silver there,' the tax collector rasped. 'Silver that will delight your heart if you lift your petticoats.'

The young woman led him on. Beatrice followed, now seriously alarmed, her own troubles forgotten. They came to the mouth of an alleyway. The wench freed herself and stood back. Goodman turned, arms outstretched.

'Come here!' He swayed on his feet. 'Come to Goodman!'

The two men who stepped out of the mouth of the alleyway were masked and cowled but the long blades they carried winked in the night. Beatrice screamed but it made difference. Goodman's assailants were upon him. He fell his knees, a knife in his back, blood spurting out of his mou He was seized by his scrawny hair and his exposed throat s from ear to ear. He collapsed on the muddy cobbles, coughi and spluttering on the blood pouring from his mouth. Th wench and the two assassins fled into the blackness of th alleyway.

Beatrice crouched beside the corpse and stared in astonis ment. Goodman was dead, his cadaver had stopped twitchin He lay, eyes open and then he was standing up, separate a distinct, the same as had happened to her. He patted his jerki his hand going to the dagger in his belt.

'What is the matter?' He saw Beatrice staring at him. F took a step forward. 'What is the matter?' he cried. 'I lie the yet I am here!'

Beatrice was frightened. She was aware of a terribl stench like that of a slaughterhouse. Goodman stagger towards her and then suddenly stopped, terrified. A da shield had appeared beside him, another to his left, o above his head. The shields clustered into a great da opening, a yawning cave, and out of this poured arm and mailed men, their armour black, their surcoats trimm blood-red. One of them glared at Beatrice. His helmet w empty, except for eyes which glowed like fiery charco Goodman screamed as these strange apparitions seized hi and dragged him into the black opening. Then they we gone. The street was silent and empty except for Goodma

Winthrop's corpse lying on the cobbles in an ever-widening pool of blood.

Beatrice hurried on. She did not want to see or experience anything else. She passed a fleshers' yard and, before she realised it, was in the herb garden behind the Golden Tabard. She walked through the wall into the deserted taproom. The tables and stools had been cleared away and the candles doused. Only a night-light, capped in the lantern horn, stood on the empty hearth. She heard the sound of weeping and went up the stairs to a small chamber which served as the parlour. Aunt Catherine and Uncle Robert were sitting in the window seat, arms round each other. Aunt Catherine's sweet face was damp with tears. Uncle Robert, barely able to cope with his own grief, sat and patted her gently on the shoulder.

'I want to go there.' Aunt Catherine got to her feet. 'We shouldn't let her corpse lie cold and alone.'

'It is the dead of night,' Uncle Robert replied gently. 'Beatrice would have understood. Her body is in good hands. Sir John Grasse will show her honour, and Father Aylred always praised her.'

'I went up to her chamber,' Aunt Catherine said, her voice catching. 'I found a garland of flowers on her bed. She must have intended to wear it this morning but she was in such a hurry, so eager to see Ralph, so determined not to be late.' Aunt Catherine put her face in her hands and sobbed. The sight of her generous-hearted aunt, loving as any mother, sitting there sobbing, her body shaking with grief, and Uncle Robert, ever practical, now not knowing what to do, was too much for Beatrice. She kissed each on the brow. 'If I could I'd break through,' she said from the bottom of her heart. 'I'd tell you not to mourn, not to grieve.' And she turned and went down the stairs, out across the moon-washed garden into the high street.

She wandered aimlessly, staring at the things she had taken for granted only a few hours earlier. At the end of the high street a light was burning in a rear window. This was Elizabeth Lockyer's cottage, a good-hearted old woman who made simples and herb poultices for those who could not afford the fees of physicians, leeches or apothecaries. A few weeks earlier Elizabeth herself had fallen ill and her life was despaired of. Now Beatrice went into the cottage and up into the bed loft to see how she was.

Elizabeth Lockyer lay with her head back against a dirty bolster, her grey hair soaked in sweat. She was alone and undoubtedly at death's door. Her skin was tight, eyelids fluttering, mouth open. She feebly stretched out a hand to reach for a cup of water but knocked it over. The water soaked the dirty horse blanket.

'All alone,' Beatrice whispered. 'Oh, Elizabeth, all alone.'

How often this old woman had gone out in the middle of the night to tend to a sick child or an expectant mother. Now she was dying in this shabby, ill-smelling bed loft without the comfort of even a priest. Beatrice crouched beside the thin straw bed. She tried to grasp the old woman's vein-streaked hand and wipe her brow. Elizabeth opened her eyes, staring up at her, smiling.

'Is it you, Beatrice? Beatrice Arrowner? I have had such strange dreams.' The words came in a rasp. 'You're a fine girl,' the old woman whispered. 'Always generous. It's good of you to come. Won't you wait, just for a while?'

'I am here,' Beatrice replied, wondering if the old woman could hear her. She crouched, the silence broken only by mice scrabbling in the corner. The end came quickly. The death rattle in the old woman's throat grew stronger, the breathing more rapid, then Elizabeth gave a great sigh and lay still.

Beatrice stared down at the corpse. Would the same thing happen as with Goodman Winthrop? She felt a blast of heat. One of the golden spheres she had seen in the castle chapel appeared out of the darkness. It spun, turning and twisting above the corpse, and grew larger. Elizabeth Lockyer's spirit, looking the same as she did on her death bed, rose. The old woman was bewildered, dazed. As she stared in confusion, the sphere of light enveloped her. It was peopled by young men and women dressed in pale green and gold, laughing and talking. Beatrice watched fascinated. The young men and women spoke to Elizabeth. Beatrice could tell by the gestures of their hands, their smiles, the way their sapphire-blue eyes twinkled that they were reassuring her and offering her comfort.

Elizabeth grew less agitated; her back straightened, the lines and wrinkles disappeared from her face, and as the years receded her hair grew longer, rich and black. The old, threadbare gown was also transmuted as this alchemy took place. Beatrice called out. Elizabeth turned and smiled but one of the figures came between her and Beatrice. The golden sphere rose, growing smaller, full of blazing light before it abruptly disappeared. Beatrice, standing alone in a tawdry chamber above a raddled, sweat-soaked corpse, felt a profound sense of desolation. Why was this happening? Had she been condemned? But what had she done in life? What wrong had she committed? Even Father Aylred had chuckled in amusement when she had gone to be shriven. 'Petty faults, Beatrice,' he had murmured. 'They make God laugh more than weep.'

Beatrice resisted the surge of fury which threatened to overtake her. She had never been prone to feel sorry for herself yet here she was, plucked from life by some foul assassin and cast adrift in this grey world. She was haunted by spectres, ghouls and phantasms, excluded from the light whose warmth she had tantalisingly felt.

She wandered out into the street. A man in tattered garments came running up; his face was pinched and leering, his neck strangely twisted. He clacked a dish and jabbered at her. Beatrice, growing accustomed to this world of spectres, ignored him and turned away.

'Beatrice! Beatrice Arrowner!'

The young woman standing near the horse trough was a vision of beauty. Golden hair hanging loose down to her shoulders framed an ivory face perfectly formed, red lips, laughing green eyes slightly slanted at the corners. She was dressed in a beautiful gown of blue and gold, with silver-toed and silver-heeled boots on her feet. A golden bracelet with silver hearts hung from one wrist, and round her neck a filigree chain held a gold disc with a red ruby in the centre.

'You are sad?' The young woman's voice was soft and musical.

'What is your name?' Beatrice snapped.

'Why, Clothilde. Do you like your new world, Beatrice?'

'No, no, I don't!'

'And your murder?'

'How do you know?' Beatrice demanded. 'How do you know about my death?'

'I saw you fall,' Clothilde replied, taking Beatrice's hand. 'I saw you fall like a star from Heaven. You know you did not slip?' She gently caressed the side of Beatrice's head. 'That terrible blow sent you spinning out of life.'

'Please don't play games with me!'

Clothilde drew even closer and Beatrice marvelled at the perfume this unexpected visitor wore. 'Don't be such a child, Beatrice. Think coolly, reflect. Why should someone want to kill young Mistress Arrowner? What enemies did you have?'

'I had none.' Beatrice looked up at the sky. It was empty now of the shifting forms and shapes. 'I had none,' she repeated. 'I cared for all my friends. I rarely had harsh words.'

'So what did you have that someone else wanted?' Clothilde asked.

'Why, nothing,' Beatrice replied. 'My aunt and uncle have no riches. I had no treasure – that's what people kill for, isn't it?'

Clothilde laughed. 'You mentioned the word treasure. You had Ralph.'

'But I had no rivals, or none that I know of,' she added in alarm.

'No, no, don't vex yourself,' Clothilde reassured her. 'But what was Ralph searching for?'

Beatrice stared into those light-green eyes. 'I met a young man,' she replied slowly. 'Do you know him? Crispin?'

Clothilde nodded.

'He said the same, that I was not supposed to die.'

'Think!' Clothilde's voice was low and urgent. 'Remember, Beatrice. You went up on to the parapet walk. You were looking for Ralph. Remember how dark it was. Someone was waiting for you in that shadowy tower.'

'But I was wearing a gown,' Beatrice protested.

'And Ralph was wearing a cloak,' Clothilde pointed out. 'All the assassin saw was a dark shape, clothes fluttering in the breeze, footsteps along the stone walk.'

'Oh no! They thought I was Ralph!' Beatrice gasped. 'They killed me because they thought I was Ralph. That means they will kill again. I must get back!'

'No, no.' Clothilde held her hands. 'Two deaths in one night, Beatrice, will provoke suspicion.'

'It's Brythnoth's treasure, isn't it? Ralph said he was close to discovering its whereabouts. Whoever killed me wanted to silence him. What can I do?' If Clothilde hadn't held her fast with a force which kept her rooted to the spot, Beatrice would have fled back to Ravenscroft.

'Hush now!' the rich, low voice soothed. 'Don't fret yourself, Mistress Arrowner. Perhaps I can help you.'

Beatrice stared at Clothilde. She had never seen such beauty, except in a painted Book of Hours Father Aylred had shown her.

'Who are you? What are you?' she asked. 'Where do you come from? Why do you want to help me?'

'Because we are alone, Beatrice, lost on the other side of death. Don't you want justice, vengeance on your killer?'

'What does it all mean?' Beatrice demanded. 'I see silver discs and golden spheres of light.' She stared across the street. Goodman Winthrop's corpse still lay sprawled at the mouth of the alleyway. 'Horrid shapes like knights in armour but with no faces, only eyes which glow in the darkness. Sometimes these shapes see me, sometimes they're just like wisps of smoke.'

'In time all will be made clear,' Clothilde replied reassuringly. 'I have lived in this world for many a year. I know it well. I can explain it. Once, many, many years ago, I was like you.'

'And what happened?' Beatrice asked.

'Never mind.' Clothilde laughed, shook her head and smoothed the golden hair away from her face. 'Killed like you, I was. Sent out into the darkness before my time. But I exacted vengeance.'

'How?' Beatrice demanded. 'We are cut off from the living by a thick, glass-like wall. They cannot see, hear or touch us, nor can we them.'

'There is a way,' came the reply. 'In time.'

'You play with me.'

'No, I don't, Beatrice. You remember Father Aylred's stories about the terrible cries from Midnight Tower? This glass wall can be penetrated but, as in life, it takes time and skill.'

'If you know so much then say who killed me.'

'I would if I could, Beatrice. But look around you. We are no different from the living. We cannot be in all places at all times.'

'And the treasure? Brythnoth's cross? Is it a fable?'

'In time that, too, can be found. Now, come with me, Beatrice.'

Beatrice hung back warily. Clothilde's beautiful face seemed a little more pointed, the even white teeth reminded her of a cat, and those green eyes were very watchful.

'Where is Goodman Winthrop?' she asked.

'Why, Beatrice, with the demons. After death the true self manifests itself. As in life so in death. But come, I wish to show you something. Questions later.' Clothide grasped Beatrice by the hand.

They moved quickly along the high street out into the country lanes. The strange bronze light was all around them. It was night yet they could see where they went. They walked but they seemed to travel faster as if borne by swift horses. Beatrice felt the ground beneath her slip away. She would stop and stare at places she recognised: a turnstile, a gate, the brow of some hill. Each had memories from her previous life. Her companion had fallen silent. Now and again she'd whisper to herself in a language Beatrice couldn't understand. The houses and farms fell away and they entered that desolate part of Essex which ran down to the estuary of the Blackwater, a bleak place even on a summer's day. Now it seemed like the heathland of Hell. Beatrice paused as they climbed the hill overlooking the water. In a small copse she glimpsed a movement. She let go of her companion's hand and went across. A beggar man, one she had seen at the Golden Tabard days earlier, was crouched beneath the bush. A piece of threadbare sacking covered his shoulders and his seamed face was dirty and coated in sweat.

'He's ill,' Beatrice declared. 'He has the same fever as Elizabeth Lockyer. Can't we help?'

Clothilde glanced up at the sky. 'Daylight will soon break.'

'So, the stories are true,' said Beatrice. 'Ghosts can only walk at night!'

Clothilde laughed deep in her throat. 'Children's tales! But the shapes I wish to show you will disappear.'

Beatrice ignored her. She peered at the beggar man and stretched out a hand to stroke his face. There was no response.

'He is dying.' Clothilde's voice was harsh. 'There is nothing we can do. Each man's fate is a line of thread which is played out to the end.'

Beatrice was full of pity. The beggar man was old, with balding pate, unkempt beard and moustache. He must have crawled out here like a dog to die.

'Life is harsh,' Clothilde murmured.

'So is death,' Beatrice retorted. 'I will not leave him. His end must be near.' She ignored the hiss of annoyance from her companion.

Beatrice remembered the words of the Requiem and recited them. A short while passed and the beggar man's shaking ceased. There was no death rattle, just a sigh and he lay still. Beatrice waited to see what would happen. The same manifestation occurred. The beggar man's shade stood beside the corpse. The old man looked up at the sky, hands beseeching in death as they did in life. No golden spheres appeared, nor those black, cavernous shapes. Instead, figures dressed like monks, hoods and cowls obscuring their faces, clustered round the deceased. They were urging him to accompany them. He was reluctant, arguing back. One of the figures passed a hand over his face as if showing him something; the beggar man fell silent and, with a figure on either side, he walked away and disappeared, leaving his dirty corpse on the heathland.

Beatrice looked at Clothilde who was standing behind her staring out towards the river, and just for a moment she thought Clothilde was Crispin. She grew frightened.

'What is happening?' she asked.

'If you want my help,' Clothilde replied, 'hurry now!' And, grasping Beatrice's hand, she led her to the brow of the hill.

Chapter 4

The mud flats of the Blackwater estuary stretched below Beatrice. She had been here before with Aunt Catherine to cut rushes, search for herbs, even catch fish. It was a desolate place where the gulls and cormorants wheeled and whined and a biting wind always seemed to blow. Now it was changed. The estuary was a battlefield. Men were hacking and cutting at each other. In the river beyond, Beatrice could see long, rakish ships, their prows carved as dragons, griffins and wolves, their sails furled. A hostile army had landed. The invaders wore steel conical helmets whose broad nose guards hid most of their faces. In the early dawn light Beatrice could see their standards; one showed a red, snarling dragon, another a huge black raven with yellow beak and talons. The men they fought were grouped round a great standard depicting a fighting man against a green and gold background. Beside this standard, crosses lashed to lances were held high in the air.

Beatrice was no soldier but she could see that the defenders were hard pressed. They were retreating inland, leaving the dead piled two or three high. The sand was red with blood and the air loud with the crash of steel against wood, cries, groans, shouted orders.

'Look.' Clothilde pointed with her finger. 'That warrior beside the Fighting Man standard is Earl Brythnoth.'

Beatrice stared fascinated at the tall, blond-haired giant surrounded by his house carls in their chain-mail byrnies. Some wore helmets, others were bareheaded. Brythnoth was gesturing with his arm, shouting orders, urging the shield wall to hold fast.

'But this happened many years ago,' Beatrice said.

'A shade of the past,' Clothilde replied. 'Now, look what is about to happen. Watch Brythnoth carefully.'

The giant earl stepped back as if he wished to distance himself from the fighting. He was talking quickly to a young man kneeling beside him. As Beatrice watched, Brythnoth took something from round his neck; the gold glinted in the light. He thrust it into the young man's hand.

'Brythnoth is giving Cerdic the holy cross,' Beatrice whispered. She clasped her hands, for a few seconds forgetting her own situation. If only Ralph was here. If he could only see what she was witnessing.

'Watch!' Clothilde plucked at her.

The young man, shield slung behind him, sword in hand, was now leaving the battlefield, climbing the hill towards them. Round his neck hung the beautiful cross. He came straight towards them, ignorant of their presence. He reminded Beatrice of Ralph with his pale face, generous mouth, large staring eyes. He was obviously exhausted. His chain mail was covered in blood and gore, cuts and scratches scored his face and hands.

He stopped on the brow of the hill and looked back, lips moving wordlessly. Beatrice stared at the cross. It was exquisitely carved with strange emblems and motifs and in the centre, above the gold crosspiece, a blood-red ruby glowed like a living flame. Cerdic took one last look at the fighting and ran down the hill towards the trackway into Maldon.

'Come, Beatrice,' said Clothilde, 'let's follow him.'

They hastened in pursuit, keeping the spectre of the long-dead soldier in view.

'Has this happened before?' Beatrice asked.

'Of course!' Clothilde replied.

'Then you must know where he hides it.'

Clothilde shook her head. 'You will see. You will see.'

At last they reached Ravenscroft Castle. It looked so familiar, so ordinary. But Cerdic was running on as if the castle didn't exist. He crossed the moat and disappeared into the barbican. They followed and found the castle bailey deserted apart from a sleepy-eyed pot boy who was letting the dogs out, and his sister, the goose girl, who was summoning her charges to take them on to the green. Beatrice forgot about the treasure and felt a deep sadness for the familiar scene.

'You must remember, Beatrice,' said Clothilde, 'that what you have seen are the shapes and shades of former things. Cerdic left the battlefield and came to Ravenscroft. However, on the day he died, no castle stood here, only a brook which is now the moat, and a wooden palisade where Brythnoth camped before marching against the invaders.' She shrugged. 'Cerdic's ghost comes here with the cross then disappears. So now you know, the treasure really exists. It lies somewhere near and Ralph could find it.'

The door to the keep flew open and Father Aylred came out. A silver and gold cloak hung from his shoulders and in his hands, covered by a white linen cloth, was the ciborium holding the Host. A boy from the castle carried a lighted candle before him.

'It's Father Aylred!' Beatrice exclaimed. 'He must be taking the viaticum to a member of the garrison who is sick. Father Aylred!' she called but the priest walked on.

'I must go.' Clothilde's voice was now a deep rasp. 'I cannot stay here!'

Beatrice looked round but her companion had disappeared. Beatrice walked to the Lion Tower. Perhaps she should go up and see Ralph.

'Christ be with you, Mistress Arrowner.'

The young man she had seen earlier in the night, with his fresh, cheerful face and spiky hair, was standing on the cobbles behind her.

'Tarry awhile.' He held his hands out.

'Why should I?' Beatrice noticed a silver disc hovering between her and the young man, then it disappeared.

He walked towards her. In the early morning light she could see that his face was a weather-beaten ruddy brown and his eyes were light blue. He was now dressed in a leather, sleeveless jerkin over a white cambric shirt, leggings of brown wool pushed into soft leather boots, a black belt round his slim waist. He drew closer. She noticed how fine his teeth were, how clean and neat he was.

'Who are you?' she asked. 'Why do you keep warning me to be careful?'

'My name is Brother Antony.'

Beatrice smiled. 'That's the name of my favourite saint, Antony of Padua, the Franciscan. Aunt Catherine has a small statue of him.'

Brother Antony laughed. 'Would you like to walk with me?'

'But who are you? Another relic of this castle?'

Antony's face grew grave. 'It doesn't matter who I am. What is really important, Beatrice, is who are you? It is important to realise that Ralph is still in great danger and so are you.'

'But I am dead,' she laughed. 'I am beyond all pain and hurt.'

'Death is not an end,' Antony replied gravely. 'It marks a new beginning. I have let you wander, now I must speak to you. I mean you well. I swear that on the wounds of Christ. Afterwards, it is up to you whether you heed my advice or not.'

'Do you know who murdered me?'

Antony shook his head. 'Only God knows that.'

'Then why doesn't God intervene?'

'But God does, Beatrice. That's why I'm here.'

'How do I know that?' she snapped, and as she spoke the castle yard changed again. Great gibbet posts rose up from the cobbles. They were about five yards high with three branches and from each bodies jerked and spluttered in their death spasms. The cruel knight was there again, seated on his black war horse, watching. Women carrying children screamed and begged for mercy but the knight and his henchmen mocked them. The victims were hustled up the ladders, nooses placed round their necks, the ladders turned and more bodies danced in the air.

'Come away! Come away!' Antony was beside her. He smelt of sweet grass and herbs.

'What is all this?' Beatrice whispered.

But Antony was leading her away, talking soothingly to her. Soon they were out of the castle, walking towards Devil's Spinney. Halfway there he stopped and sat down on the grass, gesturing at Beatrice to join him. He grasped her hands as Ralph would, rubbing them between his, watching her intently.

'I do not know who killed you, Beatrice. The assassin really intended to slay Ralph your beloved. I know that. You are truly dead, Beatrice Arrowner. There is no going back. No return to the life you have left.'

'And is this Heaven or Hell?' Beatrice asked bravely.

'This is no place, Beatrice.' He paused. 'It's like dusk, caught between night and day. Death is a journey, one that takes all eternity. If you die with your face towards God, you journey towards God and He is eternal.'

'A journey?' Beatrice queried.

Antony nodded. 'An eternal journey, but you have not yet begun on it.'

'Why not?'

'Because you don't want to leave.'

'What do you mean?' Beatrice asked.

He held out his hands, fingers splayed. 'You have intellect, love and will. The first can propose, the second can be your aim – or not, depending on yourself. The third, however, is most important. It is what determines your actions. Your will is what keeps you here. You have decided not to travel on. You have unfinished business.'

'But what about Goodman Winthrop? He was collected by those terrors.'

'He made his choice.'

'Will he travel towards God?'

'God will always call him, but if Goodman Winthrop lives his death like he lived his life, he will for all eternity refuse to hear the call and travel away from God, into his own self, his own love of wickedness. That's why he was taken by the demons. They did not come from Hell, Beatrice, they came from within himself.'

'And the poor beggar man?'

'Ah.' Antony smiled. 'The Church teaches of Heaven and Hell and I have described both to you. The Church also teaches Purgatory where the soul is undecided. No, no.' He shook his head. 'I put that wrongly, the soul is not yet prepared for the journey.'

'But that's like me.'

'No, your soul is ready but your will wants to delay because you have unfinished business which, I suspect, is connected with Master Ralph. That poor beggar man was collected by the wraiths of his mind and will, the sins and impurities he accummulated during life, for he was a beggar man by choice rather than by misfortune.'

'And Elizabeth Lockyer?'

'Ah. She was visited by the seraphims, beings of light. Elizabeth lived a good life, she died with her face towards God and God smiled on her. She wished to travel on and all the good she did in life has taken her forward.'

'Seraphims? Wraiths? Demons? What about those others? Malkyn the torturer, Lady Johanna de Mandeville, the poor unfortunate who haunts the crossroads?'

'They do not wish to travel on,' Antony explained. 'They are still locked in the pain and misery of their lives. Lady Johanna died a miserable death. God wishes to comfort her but she will not respond. Etheldreda, the young woman at the crossroads, is the same. She's no sinner, just an unfortunate young woman who died when her wits were turned.'

'And Malkyn the torturer?'

'A cruel man in life, Beatrice. He did repent before he died, he was shriven by a priest here in the castle, but he does not wish to purge himself. He will stay here until he does.'

'And those shapes and shades, spectres and ghouls?' Beatrice asked. 'That terrible knight, those men being hanged in the courtyard? And the battle?'

'They are different. They are nothing but shadows of former beings. They are like tapestries which show a scene from the past.' He sensed Beatrice's puzzlement. 'Have you ever been into a room, Beatrice, after there has been feasting and revelry? It's very quiet but if you stand and listen you can almost hear the laughter, the music, the dancing which occurred there.'

Beatrice nodded. 'But what am I to do?'

'Do you want to leave?' Antony asked quietly.

'I want to marry Ralph. I want justice for my death.'

'But that's impossible,' Antony murmured.

Beatrice sprang to her feet. 'The others didn't say that!'

'What others, Beatrice? Clothilde and Crispin?'

'Yes.' Beatrice sighed. 'I am flouncing away in a temper but what good will that do? They did offer to help.'

'And that's why I'm here.' Antony spoke sharply. 'Of all the beings you've met, Beatrice, those two are the most dangerous!'

He spoke so vehemently, Beatrice sat down again. 'Who are they?'

'They are one and the same person,' Antony replied. 'Succubus and Incubus.'

'What?'

'They are the true devils,' Antony warned.

'But they were so beautiful, so helpful.'

'Haven't you heard the old phrase, Beatrice, "The Devil can appear as an angel of light"?' He grasped her hands. 'When Goodman Winthrop died, you saw demons, but they came from within. They were of his own making, his lusts, his avarice and desire for power.'

'Did he kill that young girl?' Beatrice asked. 'Phoebe? Where is she and why can't I see her spirit?'

Antony smiled. 'Phoebe has gone on; her death cannot be laid at Goodman Winthrop's door. In life, as in death, nothing is what it seems. Oh, listen to me, Beatrice! There is a difference between the demons we create and those devils, those fallen angels who constantly rage against the light, who would, if they could, scale the walls of Heaven and burn them to the ground.'

'I don't believe you.' Beatrice withdrew her hands, yet she could tell from Antony's eyes that he was deeply worried.

'What do you expect devils to be like, Beatrice? Little men with forked tails and horns? Creatures from some mummers' play?' he scoffed. 'They are nothing but lurid paintings. Devils are like angels, Beatrice, a mixture of pure light, energy, intelligence and will. They can take on many forms and guises.'

'But I am dead. Holy Mother Church teaches that after death comes judgement.' She shook her head. 'Why should they be interested in my soul now?'

'Oh, they are, Beatrice. Very, very interested, especially in one like you. You have not yet travelled on. You are capable of free choice. You are here because you want to be. You have not journeyed on because you have refused to. In a way, you are no different from Malkyn or Lady Johanna de Mandeville, so the angels of Hell are interested in you, deeply interested.

If they can, they will turn your will so your face no longer looks towards God.'

'Is that what is happening to Malkyn and the rest?' she asked.

'Yes, it is. That's what Satan and all his armies want. A shattering of harmony, the breakdown of peace, misery and tribulation. The capture of souls.'

'But if I have a will, why can't I . . .'

'Intervene? Cross to the other side? You could.'

'I can.' Beatrice smiled.

'You have intellect, you have will,' Antony went on cautiously. 'And that's the supreme temptation.'

'You mean, if I obey Crispin and Clothilde?'

'They will give you that power for a price.'

'And can't the beings of light?'

'They can, Beatrice, but it has to be earned.'

A silver disc came between them and moved away.

'What is that?' Beatrice asked.

Antony did not answer.

'Are Crispin and Clothilde my guardian devils?' Beatrice asked.

'They are one and the same,' Antony repeated. 'Succubus and Incubus, the male and female face of a fallen angel. They can appear in many forms, many guises. They can laugh and tease, they can rage and plot.'

Beatrice stared up at the sky. It was blue but tinged with that strange bronze coppery light. Shapes and shades were moving across like a flock of geese, dark and forbidding.

'What are they?'

'The Devil's huntsmen.' Antony narrowed his eyes. 'They streak across the world seeking their quarry. And to answer your question, Beatrice, yes, Crispin and Clothilde are your guardian devil.'

'And where is my guardian angel?'

'The silver disc,' he replied. 'I can only tell you so much.' His voice grew weaker. 'In the end, Beatrice, you must make your own choices. I can help if you wish but in the end only you can decide.' He held up three fingers. 'Intellect, love and will. You can force anyone to do anything but you cannot force someone to love. God's love is eternal, it is like that of a loving mother. God wants that love returned, freely, without hindrance.' Antony got to his feet and helped her up. 'He loves you, Beatrice, but you have to decide. Remember the words of scripture: "You cannot have two masters."'

'But I haven't seen God. I am here by myself.'

'No, you are not, Beatrice. You are not alone. And you do see God. You see Him in the faces of those around you.' He held both her hands and drew her close.

Beatrice felt strange; she was out on this bronze-coloured heath, the castle behind her, those eerie shapes scurrying across the sky above her. She only wished Ralph was here, not this strange young man. If Ralph were here she could travel on. If Ralph died, they'd be together. As that strange thought began to turn and twist, she saw the sad look in Antony's eyes.

'Don't think that, Beatrice,' he whispered. 'The lover always wishes the best for the loved.'

Beatrice glanced away.

'Remember what I have said. Remember the warnings I have given you. Let me tell you something else. As you travel this world, as you cross from one existence to another, be careful of those who seem to be angels of light.'

'How will I know the difference?'

'How do you know an apple tree?' He countered, and answered his own riddle. 'By the fruit it bears.'

Beatrice started at the terrible howling of a dog, followed by terrible cries from Devil's Spinney.

'I must go.' Antony smiled. 'But I shall return. I shall watch you, Beatrice, and, when I can, I will help. But in the end all decisions must be yours.' He passed a hand over his face, gently stretched forward and patted her cheek. His eyes were sad. 'You have so much light in you, so much power. Don't let it be turned. Beware. Crispin and Clothilde are what they are but, in your travels, be most careful of the Minstrel Man.'

'The Minstrel Man?'

'You will meet him.' Antony was now moving away.

'The Minstrel Man?'

'That's what he calls himself,' Antony replied. 'He knows you are here, Beatrice, and he'll come looking for you. You are a great prize. You are not as lonely as you think. Farewell, Beatrice!'

The silver disc of light appeared between them and Antony was gone.

Beatrice rose and walked towards Devil's Spinney. She went into the trees, moving without effort through the undergrowth; the brambles and weeds proved no hindrance. At last she found herself in the grove, a small glade in the centre, fringed by seven great oaks. She had been here on many occasions with Ralph; they'd lie in the soft grass and plan their future lives. Beatrice again felt that terrible surge of rage like a tongue of fire through her whole being. She crouched down, stared across the glade and blinked. She was not alone.

Men, old and grizzled, grey beards reaching down beneath their stomachs, their heads garlanded with wreaths, stood beneath an oak tree. They were garbed from head to toe in dirty white robes. They carried sickle-shaped knives and were staring up into the branches. Beatrice felt a chill of fear and started in alarm as a naked body crashed from the branches only to jerk and dangle on the rope tied round its neck. Beatrice stared in disgust. The man was naked except for a loin cloth. He choked and kicked as the ancient priests, following some bloodthirsty ritual, lifted their hands and chanted to the skies. The grisly scene provoked memories of what Ralph had told her about this place. He used to frighten her, in a teasing way, when he described the pagan priests who would meet here to sacrifice victims to their pagan god of the oak.

Beatrice was watching a phantasm but the horror repelled her. She wished, despite what Antony had said, that Crispin or Clothilde were here.

Words Between the Pilgrims

The clerk of Oxford paused in his tale and stared at the faces, tense and watchful in the firelight.

'Would you fill my stoup with ale?'

The miller hastened to obey.

The summoner, his pimples even brighter in the firelight, staggered to his feet and stared across at the clerk. 'How do you know all this?'

'He didn't say it was true,' the squire pointed out.

'Well, is it true?' the summoner demanded, his voice shrill.

'It depends,' said the clerk, 'what you mean by true.'

'That's no answer,' the summoner replied aggressively.

The clerk stared across at their leader. Sir Godfrey was studying him closely. The knight did not wish to intervene even though he was a man who had experienced the twilight world of demons. He had hunted the murderous blood-drinkers scattered throughout Europe from the shores of the Bosphorus to the cold, icy wastes of Norway. Yet that was his personal struggle. He was also special emissary for the Crown and the Archbishop of Canterbury and often attended hushed, closed meetings in certain chambers at the House of Secrets in London. Beside him his son, the squire, stirred.

'Father,' he whispered. 'Weren't you sent to Ravenscroft Castle?'

'Hush now,' his father responded.

He sat and listened as the summoner continued to question the clerk. For some strange reason the summoner seemed most perturbed by the story. The knight smiled grimly to himself. His son was right, he had been sent to Ravenscroft Castle, and it was only a matter of time before someone recognised the name Goodman Winthrop. After all, the tax collector had been the scourge of the southern shires.

The taverner raised his fat, cheery face. 'Sir!' he shouted at the summoner. 'Will you shut up!' He stretched out his hands towards the flames. 'I know of Ravenscroft Castle and I also know of two people called Robert and Catherine Arrowner who owned a tavern named the Golden Tabard.'

'But if the tale is true,' the pardoner exclaimed, 'it concerns us. Good ladies, gentle sirs, look around you.'

They did so, staring into the mist-cloying darkness.

'The miller said this place was haunted,' the pardoner continued. 'Does that mean the dead are all around us now?'

'Oh, spare the thought and don't tickle my imagination!' the wife of Bath squeaked. She just wished she hadn't turned away from the flames. The trees stood like menacing sentinels around them. And that mist! Did it bring more to this silent grove than just the cold night air?

'It could be true,' the prioress's priest spoke up. Usually this handsome, florid-faced man kept his own counsel. 'I believe death is like entering a mansion house; each chamber is full of new worlds.' He smiled at the clerk. 'I am much taken by your description, sir.' He paused as an owl hooted. 'And before this night is done, perhaps you'll be kind enough to tell us where this story came from.'

'Perhaps I will,' the clerk muttered. 'But listen now, gentle sirs and ladies. True, the darkness is deep, a mist has swirled in through the trees and the owl keeps its lonely vigil. Yet these are not real terrors.' He glanced away. 'Not like the ones to come.'

PART II

Chapter 1

Ralph Mortimer sat in Devil's Spinney, his back to an oak tree. He watched a squirrel clamber between fallen branches and scrabble up the trunk of one of the ancient oaks. Ralph wiped the tears from his eyes and pushed the wineskin away.

'I've drunk enough,' he muttered. 'And that's no help.'

A few hours earlier he had attended Beatrice's funeral in the small cemetery in the far corner of the castle near the rabbit warren. Her aunt and uncle had attended, Theobald Vavasour, Adam and Marisa, and of course Sir John Grasse and Lady Anne. Father Aylred had sung the Requiem Mass and then the corpse had been taken out on a bier and lowered into the shallow grave. The carpenter had put together a crude cross and Sir John had solemnly promised that it would be replaced, within the month, by a stone plinth bearing Beatrice's name.

It was only when the grave was being filled in that Ralph had fully understood what was happening. Beatrice was gone.

He would never see her again: those beautiful eyes, the merry mouth, her endearing mannerisms. Above all, her presence, warm and loving, like stepping out into the sunshine and basking in its golden warmth. Sometimes, in his chamber, he smelt her perfume – Beatrice had kept some there and unable to bear the reminder he'd given it to Marisa.

Ralph, who had studied all forms of knowledge at the Halls of Cambridge, could not come to terms with his grief. Deep in his heart he felt a devastating loneliness, a savage hurt which would not heal. Adam and Marisa had been helpful. Father Aylred had tried to give words of comfort but it was to no avail. The more they spoke, the more intense the pain flared.

'What can I do?' Ralph whispered. He stared up at the interlacing branches. The weather had turned cold, dark clouds scudded in to block out the sun. 'If I drink, I become sottish. If I work, my mind becomes distracted.' He beat his fist against his thigh. 'Why?' he screamed, his voice echoing round the empty glade. 'Why, Beatrice, did you climb the parapet walk at night?'

Doubts pushed away his grief, and allowed reason to surface. Beatrice was not frightened of heights. She had often walked along the parapet at the dead of night. She knew the dangers. She was safe as long as she kept to the wall. The night had been calm. No rain or wind. So how had she fallen? He recalled her corpse, laid out in its coffin before the chapel altar. Lady Anne and her tiring-women had done their best to dress the body for burial. Ralph had inspected the wounds and bruises most closely. The terrible fall had left its mark. Father Aylred, however, had whispered about the great bruise on the right side of Beatrice's head. Had that occurred before the fall? The priest seemed agitated so Ralph had questioned him.

'Why, Father, do you think it is significant?'

They had been standing alone in the small sacristy. Father Aylred put his fingers to his lips; he closed the door, turning the key in the lock.

'I am just worried, Ralph.' The little priest's face was pale and unshaven. 'Nightmares plague my sleep; I am troubled by doubts and worries.'

Ralph had only half listened, eager to return and sit beside the coffin before the lid was sealed for ever. 'Father, this is not the time or the place.'

'No, no, it isn't.' And the priest picked up a pruning knife to trim one of the purple candles for the Requiem Mass.

Ralph pulled his cloak firmly about him. The grove was dark, it looked threatening. He half smiled as he recalled the frightening stories he had told Beatrice, more the work of his imagination than anything else. He heard a twig snap and whirled round. Someone was in the trees behind him.

'Who's there?' he called.

'Ralph!' His name came in a loud whisper.

The clerk felt the hair on his neck curl with fear. He scrambled to his feet, his hand going to the knife in his belt. He peered through the gloom. The trees were so close

81

together, the brambles and gorse sprouted high. Were his wits wandering?

Ralph cursed the wine he had drunk; he felt unsteady on his feet, slightly sick. He should leave here. The castle was already in uproar. Goodman Winthrop's corpse had been brought back on a cart. The tax collector's clothing was drenched in blood from the gaping wounds to his back and throat. Sir John had muttered about rebels and miscreants, and loudly cursed the stupidity of the tax collector for wandering alone around the taverns and ale-houses of Maldon. He'd sent urgent messages to London; the barons of the Exchequer would not be pleased, commissioners and soldiers would be sent. Sir John Grasse would feel their wrath until the killers were brought to justice. Were these same assassins in Devil's Spinney now? wondered Ralph. A jay flew up in a flurry of black and white feathers. He must not stand like a maudlin sot; his grief, like his hands and his feet, were now part of him and he would have to bear it.

Ralph picked up the wineskin and, whirling it round his head, threw it into the undergrowth. As he staggered back along the trackway leading out on to the heathland, he quietly cursed his foolishness. 'You should be careful what you drink,' Beatrice had always warned him. 'You do not have a strong head for ale or wine.'

The clerk paused, closing his eyes against the hot tears which threatened.

'If you were only here, Beatrice! If you were only here, I'd let you nag me until the end of time!'

He stumbled on. The spinney was quiet, even the birdsong had died. Ralph recalled the stories and legends about the place. Wasn't it near here that little Phoebe had been found murdered? He hurried on. His foot caught on something and he crashed to the ground. He twisted over, and even as he did, the club caught him on the side of the head. Ralph did not lose consciousness though the pain was intense. He struggled to get up but a kick to the stomach winded him and he collapsed, his face scored by the pebbled trackway. He was dragged, his cloak being used like a rope, tightening round his neck. He couldn't resist. He was aware of brambles and briars ripping his hose. A boot came off. He tried to struggle but couldn't. He was pushed, his body rolled, then he felt the ground beneath him give way. Was he dreaming? Was he falling? He tried to concentrate, to ignore the pain. He kicked out with his legs but it was hard. He stared down and noticed green slime oozing over his thighs. He had been knocked on the head and dragged only a few yards to one of the treacherous mires, the small but deep marshes which peppered Devil's Spinney. The shock brought him to his senses. He was sinking. He flailed about, screaming and yelling.

'Ah, sweet Jesu miserere!' he prayed.

He remembered that the more he struggled, the quicker he'd sink. He tried to calm his mind, allow his body to float. He managed to turn over but the movement took him down a little further. The thick green mud was now pulling at his body as if invisible hands at the bottom of the marsh were clutching at him.

Ralph tried to ignore the pain, stretching his arms out to grasp the branches of a bush growing near the mire. He flung himself forward but the bush seemed to have a life of its own. His fingers missed. The mire crept above his stomach. Ralph was conscious of sounds, strange noises; the sky was turning an eerie bronze. He lunged again, his hand caught the bush.

'Oh, please!' he prayed. 'Please, God, don't break!'

The bush was old and tough, it took his weight. Slowly but surely, Ralph pulled himself towards it, ignoring the pain. Then he was beneath it, grasping the broad stem. He pulled himself out, almost grateful for the way the harsh branches cut and marked him. At least he was alive. The bush had saved his life. He crawled up through the undergrowth then rolled on his side and stared back. The mire was now peaceful again, the green surface unmarked, its treacherous depths hidden.

Ralph lay sobbing for a while before pulling himself to his feet. His whole body ached. He was missing one boot, the other was so muddy he took it off and threw it into the trees. He touched his still-bleeding face and felt his head where the assailant had struck him. He staggered along the path and out on to the heathland.

Beardsmore saw him first. Before Ralph had reached the drawbridge, Sir John Grasse, Father Aylred and Theobald Vavasour, accompanied by soldiers, hastened out to meet him.

'I was attacked,' Ralph stammered. 'I don't know who. In Devil's Spinney. I was thrown into the mire.'

Sir John shouted out orders. Father Aylred helped Ralph

across the bailey. They placed him in the guestroom. Father Aylred talked to him as if he was a child, pulling off his muddy clothes. Theobald helped. They washed away the mud from the cuts and bruises. The physician pushed a cup between his lips.

'Drink,' he urged. 'Drink and then you will feel better.'

Ralph obeyed. He was aware of Adam coming into the room, Marisa behind him.

'We heard what happened, Ralph. I was in the herb garden with Marisa.'

'They tried to kill me,' Ralph whispered. He felt his eyes grow heavy and he drifted into a deep sleep.

Later that day, as darkness fell, Ralph washed and dressed in new clothes, and joined the others in the great hall of the castle. He found the room more sombre than usual with its heavy hammer-beam roof and the axes, hauberks and shields nailed to the wall. The long trestle tables were bare, but glowing braziers kept the chill away and hunting dogs snouted among the rushes for scraps of food.

Sir John gathered everyone round the high table on the dais. Cold meats, bread, cheese and jugs of ale were served. The company included Sir John, his wife, the huge, burly sergeant-at-arms Stephen Beardsmore, Theobald Vavasour, Adam and Marisa, the captain of the watch and Ralph. Father Aylred hastened in and said grace; the food was distributed, the jugs circulated. Sir John, bowing to etiquette, allowed them to satisfy their hunger before tapping on the table with the hilt of his dagger.

'We live in troublesome times,' he began. 'A castle wench, Phoebe, has been murdered, her corpse found in Devil's Spinney. God rest her.'

His words were greeted with a chorus of assent.

'And with Ralph we mourn the sad death of Beatrice,' he continued, 'but now we have other more pressing matters to consider. Goodman Winthrop's corpse lies sheeted, ready for burial. He wasn't the pleasantest of companions, a boor, a sot, but he was still a royal official. Last night he was stabbed to death in Maldon. We know he left a tavern with a wench. Master Beardsmore, you and Ralph will investigate that matter tomorrow.'

'Which tavern?' the sergeant-at-arms asked.

'The Pot of Thyme. I have no doubt that Winthrop's murder is a symptom of the deep unrest caused by the poll tax. However, the King's Council in London are obdurate. Archbishop Sudbury and Hailes the treasurer are determined that the Exchequer be filled and the poll tax will go ahead. I have sent urgent missives to London. God knows what will happen now.'

'And the attack on our young clerk here,' said Lady Anne. 'Do you believe that is also linked to the tax?'

Sir John nodded, scratching his vein-streaked cheek.

Ralph put his piece of bread down. 'I don't think so. How did they know I was a member of the castle? And, even if they did, why should they attack me? I am not a tax collector.'

'I agree.' Beardsmore spoke up. The gruff sergeant-at-arms pushed his platter away. 'True, rebels are active all through

Kent and Essex but why should they attack Master Ralph the way they did? That's not their manner. More an arrow from a tree or a knife in the back.'

His words chilled Ralph and created a sombre silence.

'Do you know what you are saying?' Sir John asked carefully.

'Yes, I do.' Beardsmore was firm. 'Sir John, I am your sergeant-at-arms. My job is to defend this castle and those within it. Goodman Winthrop was undoubtedly killed by peasant rebels. Tomorrow we'll go down and turn the Pot of Thyme on its head and see what muck spills out.'

Ralph smiled at Beardsmore's bluntness. The gruff soldier usually kept his own counsel, but young Phoebe's murder still haunted him.

'You were sweet on Phoebe, weren't you?' The words were out before Ralph could think.

The sergeant-at-arms tugged at the laces on his boiled leather jerkin. 'I was more than sweet on her, Master Ralph,' he murmured, 'and over the last few days I have been thinking.'

'Then let us know what you have been thinking,' said Lady Anne.

'The night Phoebe was murdered,' Beardsmore replied, 'she wasn't supposed to be going home. She had agreed to meet me near Midnight Tower. Now, Sir John, Phoebe was a good girl. Sometimes her wits were not as sharp as they should be but she had common sense.' He paused to take a drink from his tankard.

Ralph felt a bond with this gruff soldier who had also lost a loved one yet hid his grief so well.

'Phoebe never left this castle,' Beardsmore went on. 'She wasn't stupid. Oh, some of the lads teased her but she could look after herself. She told me how Winthrop the tax collector had offered her a silver piece to lie with him.' He clenched his fist. 'I was going to have words with him.' He blinked back the tears that filled his eyes. 'In the gathering dusk she would never have gone to a place like Devil's Spinney. I believe she was murdered in Ravenscroft and her body taken out there. Physician Vavasour, you examined Phoebe's corpse. Had she been raped?'

Theobald, who had been pushing pieces of bread around on his trauncher, looked up like a frightened rabbit, eyes blinking, lips puckered.

'No, she hadn't. She had been beaten about the head before she was slain.'

Father Aylred frowned. 'But why? If she wasn't raped? She was poor, she had no silver or gold. Moreover, if she was murdered here, why didn't anyone hear her cries? And you can't just pick up a corpse and take it out across the drawbridge without being noticed.'

A murmur of assent greeted his words. Lady Anne, seated next to her husband, pushed her greying hair under the tight coif round her face. She nervously scratched her cheek and tapped the table with her fingers. 'Thank God the servants are not here.' She stared round the hall. 'Only a few days ago we all celebrated May Day. Lent and winter were behind us. There was fresh meat from the fleshers' yard, spring vegetables, herbs and flowers.' She shivered. 'But now it's like the dead of winter. Master Beardsmore,' her voice grew harsh, 'you seem to be saying there's a killer in this castle. Do you know anybody who would want to murder Phoebe?'

Before Beardsmore could reply, Father Aylred spoke up. 'As you say, Master Beardsmore, Phoebe was a good girl, a merry wench. But we all know Phoebe was curious.'

'I agree, Father.' Beardsmore's eyes fell away.

'She was more than that,' Lady Anne declared. 'She liked listening at keyholes, spying on people.'

'That's right,' Sir John agreed. 'Last year on the feast of All Souls one of the kitchen wenches had a furious argument with her. She accused Phoebe of spying on her when she was in the stable with one of the grooms.'

'Ah, yes.' Theobald held up a bony finger. 'I remember her doing that.'

'Where are the groom and wench now?' Ralph asked.

'Gone,' Beardsmore said thinly. 'They left after the Epiphany. I sided with Phoebe, that's how I first met her.'

Ralph's attention was caught by shadows dancing on the wall. Darkness had fallen swiftly and seemed to be closing in around them, despite the cresset torches and candles. The killer was in this castle. He glanced at Father Aylred, telling him with his eyes to keep his own counsel.

'What shall we do?' Lady Anne asked.

Sir John looked at Adam. 'You are our principal clerk. What do you advise?'

Adam cleared his throat. 'I agree with what has been said. Goodman Winthrop's death is the work of rebels. The attack on Ralph, however, was not the work of some peasant.'

'Is it possible,' asked Marisa, 'that the rebels have an accomplice here in the castle?'

They all looked at the petite, usually quiet young woman.

'After all,' Marisa continued, spots of excitement high in her cheeks, 'Ravenscroft defends the Blackwater estuary and the northern approaches to London. If the peasants are planning a revolt, they will want to seize it.'

'And how vital was Phoebe to the defence of this castle?' Lady Anne tried, and failed, to keep the sneer from her voice.

'Don't mock Marisa!' Adam retorted heatedly. 'What she says is possible.'

The atmosphere in the hall grew tense. Lady Anne, unused to such sharp reproofs, glared at her husband.

'Both of you could be correct,' Ralph intervened, eager to keep the peace. 'It's possible that the rebels do have supporters here among the garrison. What better way to weaken our defences than indiscriminate killings and attacks which provoke suspicion and bitter acrimony?'

Everybody seized on his explanation. Ravenscroft was a happy, amiable garrison. The castle had numerous spacious chambers which allowed people a degree of privacy, and relationships with the townspeople were usually cordial. Ralph was afraid this would soon change. Sir John smiled gratefully at him. He repeated his orders about Beardsmore and Ralph investigating Winthrop's death and ordered guards to be doubled on the barbican.

'From now on,' he concluded, 'the drawbridge will be winched up at dusk, the portcullis lowered. I want beacon lights on each rampart along the walls. No one is to enter between dusk and dawn without my permission. Now.' He pushed back his chair. 'I think enough has been said.'

The meeting broke up. Ralph, still feeling sore and shaken, walked out of the hall and sat on the steps. Adam and Marisa came and sat on either side of him. Ralph felt the warmth of their friendship.

'You didn't really mean that, did you, Ralph?' Marisa clasped his left hand, rubbing it gently between hers.

'Am I so easy to see through?' Ralph asked with a smile.

'You never were a good liar.' Adam's blue eyes twinkled in amusement. 'What do you really think happened?'

'I believe Phoebe was murdered here.'

'But how was her corpse taken out?' Marisa asked.

'There's the postern gate,' Ralph pointed out.

'But that's been closed and locked for years.'

'It can still be opened and there's a small wooden bridge across the moat. Don't forget, the postern gate lies at the rear of the castle. Sir John is a benevolent constable. He never puts guards along the ramparts unless he has to.'

'But still,' said Marisa, 'that means someone had to carry a bloody corpse across the yard. And the hinge to the gate is so rusty it would scream like a ghost.'

'Well, there's one way to find out.' Ralph got to his feet.

They left the inner bailey, passed the keep and went through the small orchard which stood in a corner of the castle. On the way, Adam lit a cresset torch. When they reached the postern gate, Ralph took one look and realised he was wrong. The gate was small and narrow, fashioned out of thick oak reinforced by metal bands and steel studs. Its two huge bolts were secure and the gate was padlocked in three places. From the rust on both the locks and the bolts, it would have been easier to knock a hole in the wall than to open the gate. Adam doused the pitch torch in a water butt, threw it down and beckoned Ralph and Marisa to follow him back into the trees.

'What now, Ralph?' he asked. 'The castle has only two entrances, the barbican and the postern gate. You have examined the latter. It has not been opened for years.'

'What about a cart or barrow?' Marisa suggested. 'Phoebe's assassin could have hidden the corpse in one of them and covered it with a sheet.'

'I doubt that,' a voice called from the darkness.

Ralph started. Beardsmore came slipping like a shadow through the trees towards them.

'I'm sorry to startle you.' The soldier cradled his conical helmet in his arms. 'I saw the torchlight and I wondered what was happening. I am not like Phoebe.' He smiled thinly. 'I examined the postern gate the morning after Phoebe's murder. I also inquired about the keys of Sir John but he doesn't even know where they are.'

'Why are you so sure that the killer didn't smuggle Phoebe's corpse out in a cart or barrow?' Adam asked, then shook his head. 'Of course, on the night Phoebe was killed you were on duty.'

'From three o'clock in the afternoon till nine,' said Beardsmore, 'I played dice with the lads in the guardhouse a couple of times but I tell you this, sirs, no one left the castle that day. If they had, I would have already brought them in for questioning.'

'And you are sure Phoebe never left?' Ralph asked.

'Not unless she could sprout wings and fly!'

Ralph studied the soldier closely. Beardsmore was actually much younger than he appeared at first glance. He had a thick, square face with close, deep-set eyes, and a jutting nose above a harsh mouth. He was clean-shaven, his hair closely cropped. Ralph recalled that he had served with Sir John both at sea and in Gascony.

Beardsmore put his helmet on. 'Now, I've got duties to attend to.' The sergeant-at-arms walked away into the darkness.

'Now, there's a strange fellow,' Adam said softly. 'Notice how quietly he moves.'

'What are you saying?' Ralph asked.

'He was on guard the night Phoebe died yet he has just assured us that she never left. But she must have done, one way or the other. How do we know he didn't let Phoebe run out and offer to meet her in Devil's Spinney? Maybe they argued, he became angry . . .'

Ralph looked at the thin sliver of moon visible through the branches. He felt cold and lonely. He missed Beatrice dreadfully. Yet there was something else now. A deep suspicion that she had not slipped but been murdered. Was his friend right? Was Beardsmore the killer?

As if she could read his thoughts, Marisa plucked at his sleeve. 'He was also on guard duty the night Beatrice fell. Maybe she saw something.'

Ralph sucked in his lips. 'And where was everybody when I was attacked in Devil's Spinney?' He glanced at Adam. 'Beardsmore was the first to see me. Is that because he had just returned?'

'I don't know,' Adam replied. 'Marisa and I were in the herb garden.'

'You should take care.' Marisa clasped his hand.

'Oh, I will.' But even as he uttered the words, Ralph knew he wasn't as fearless as he sounded.

Chapter 2

Ralph sat alone in his round chamber in the Lion Tower which stood near the barbican on the north-facing wall. He'd lit a rushlight and two candles and wondered whether he should fire the brazier, for the night had turned cold. He went across and secured the shutters. He sat at his desk, peering down at the sheaf of manuscripts which had once meant so much – the fruit of his studies and searches for Brythnoth's cross. Ralph had been born in Maldon, educated in the parish school. His father, a prosperous weaver, had secured the patronage of a local priest and sent his only son to the cathedral school at Ely before he entered the Halls of Cambridge. Ralph would always love Maldon. He had hunted wild ducks in the marshes, played outlaws with the other boys in Devil's Spinney and gone down to the Blackwater estuary to re-enact the battle of Brythnoth against the Danes.

It was old Father Dominic who had first told him about the treasure, recounting tales he himself had heard many years earlier and showing him old and tattered manuscripts about the battle. At Cambridge Ralph had pursued his searches and learnt about the flight of the squire Cerdic and those memorable words about the treasure being hidden 'on an altar to your God and mine'.

Ralph picked up a quill and tapped it against his cheek. What did the words mean? He stared at his chancery desk. He remembered how he had left everything this morning. He was punctilious in his work and particular about how he left his desk. The manuscript was askew and the ink horn and pumice stones had been moved. What could it mean?

He went and checked his coffer but the purse of silver and bronze coins had not been disturbed, and nor had his precious books, bound in vellum, on a closed shelf high on the wall. Ralph poured himself a goblet of wine to ease the pain in the back of his head.

'There can be only one conclusion,' he murmured. 'Whoever came here did not come to rob but to search.'

The only really valuable thing he owned was this battered manuscript written in his own cipher.

'They think I'm close to the treasure,' he whispered to the crucifix fastened on the wall.

A wave of nausea gripped his stomach so he went and lay on the bed. He thought of the feasting on May Day and his stupid boast about the treasure. He should have been on the parapet walk, not Beatrice. Father Aylred was right. The blow to Beatrice's head was dealt before she fell; the assassin thought he was striking at Ralph. In the dark he would only have had a few seconds to see a shadow approach the tower door. And this morning? If he'd been killed, his corpse would have been dragged out of the mire, the result of a tragic accident. People would have thought he had been drunk, as indeed he was, distraught with grief, and wandered off the trackway. And what about Phoebe? Had she been killed because she had overheard something? But how had they taken her corpse from the castle? Unless it was Beardsmore. Ralph breathed in and started. He could smell Beatrice's perfume, faint but still perceptible. Why was that? He heard a rap on the door, stretched across to his war belt and took out the dagger.

'Come in!' he called.

Father Aylred entered. Ralph relaxed and shamedfacedly threw the dagger down.

The priest shook his hand. 'I do not blame you for that, Ralph.' He came closer, his eyes sad. 'There is an assassin in our castle. He or she slew Beatrice, killed Phoebe and, this morning, tried to murder you. I've been to see old Vavasour. He confirms Beatrice could have been struck before she fell.'

Ralph rose and led the old priest across to the bed and made him sit down.

'You'll have some wine, Father?'

'Have you checked it first?'

Ralph repressed a shiver; the gentle old priest had a stubborn look.

'For the love of God, Ralph, someone tried to kill you this morning! Don't you think they'll try again?'

Ralph sniffed at the wine. 'If it's poisoned, I've already

drunk half a cup but I'll heed your warning, Father.' He sat next to the priest. 'You really do believe someone is hunting my life?'

'Worse than that, Ralph. Someone is hunting our souls!'

'Oh come, Father. Old stories about ghosts and ghouls.' He watched the candle flame suddenly dance as if a door had been opened and he sniffed the air. For a few fleeting seconds he again caught Beatrice's fragrance, soft and warm. My wits are wandering! Ralph Mortimer, you are a scholar from the Halls of Cambridge. An eternal gulf lies fixed between life and death. This old priest, with his wild accusations, is filled with superstition.

Father Aylred blessed his wine and took a sip. 'I am a peasant born and bred, Ralph.' He rolled the cup between his hands. 'My fingers are stubby and engrained with dirt. I can read sufficiently well to understand the scriptures and to preach. I put my trust in Christ the Divine Boy. I try and preach his love.'

'You are a good priest.' Ralph gripped his companion's shoulder.

'Flattery is only half the truth.' Aylred smiled. 'I can read your mind, Ralph Mortimer. You think I'm slightly fey-witted, don't you? And, by the time I am finished, you may well believe it. Look around the room, Ralph.'

Ralph obeyed.

'What do you see?'

'Light and shadows, pieces of furniture, the enclave where the window is, the shutters.'

'Our world is like that,' said Father Aylred. 'It's full of light and shadows. But, how do you know, Ralph, that someone else isn't here? Have you carefully checked?'

'No, of course, I haven't.'

'And what of the other world? The spiritual world? How do we know, Ralph, when something else has entered to wreak havoc and cause great evil?'

'Do you think that's happening at Ravenscroft?'

'Yes, I do. Read the Bible. The first real sin was that of Cain, the assassin, slaying his brother. Murder is a terrible sin, Ralph. It opens the gateways between our world and the powers of Hell. It is the abnegation of all love. A direct confrontation with God. There have been at least two murders at Ravenscroft.'

'At least?' Ralph interrupted.

'Yes. There could have been three. Now, I don't know the full reason why, but the attack on Beatrice was meant for you, I'm sure of it. Ralph, you are a good clerk. Before Beatrice's death you were investigating the legends about Brythnoth's cross. Perhaps it had something to do with that. What hour is it, please?'

Ralph walked to where an hour candle glowed faintly under its copper hood. He peered closely.

'Shortly before midnight. Why do you ask?'

'Come with me.' The priest got to his feet and walked to the door. He glanced over his shoulder. 'Please, Ralph, come with me.'

Ralph sighed, grabbed his war belt and cloak and followed

Father Aylred down the spiral staircase. The castle bailey was empty; a dog came out snarling but recognised them and slunk away. From the parapets Ralph saw the glow of braziers and torches, the shadows of sentries. Sir John's instructions were being carried out.

'It's too late,' the priest whispered, following his gaze. 'The enemy is within.'

He hastened across to Midnight Tower. A cold wind tugged at Ralph's hair and he regretted coming. He felt deeply uneasy, wary of the shadows. Ravenscroft was no longer a friendly place. Did the assassin even now peer at them from the darkness? And what did the old priest mean by the powers of Hell?

Father Aylred opened the door. As soon as he stepped inside, Ralph flinched: the tower was cold, freezing, as if this was the depths of winter and all the shutters had been opened, and the stench was as rotten as that from the moat in the height of summer; it made him gag.

'It's getting worse, Ralph.' Father Aylred's face was pallid and sweat-soaked. 'Over the last few days this freezing cold and the terrible odour has increased.' He grasped Ralph's wrists and they stood like two frightened boys.

Ralph noticed how the flames of the sconce torches flickered as if the pitch and tar were thin. Usually they gave a robust fiery glow; now the flames were weak with a strange blue tint.

'In God's name!' Father Aylred called out.

A deep sigh answered his words. Ralph felt the hair on the

nape of his neck curl, his legs tremble; he felt sick, and as weak as he was after the attack earlier today.

The priest led him up the spiral staircase, and the stench grew weaker, the cold less intense. On the first stairwell, they paused. Father Aylred crouched down against the wall, his breath coming in loud rasps.

'Every night the evil waxes stronger,' he declared. 'Each time, more and more of this tower falls under its control.'

'Can't you bless the place?' Ralph asked.

'I am just a simple country priest, Ralph. Hush now, listen!'

Ralph heard the door at the bottom of the tower open and slam shut. Someone, a knight in armour by the sound, started climbing the stairs. Ralph drew his dagger.

'It's not what you think, Ralph,' Father Aylred murmured.

As if by magic, the sound of mailed feet disappeared. Ralph went to investigate. A hideous shriek echoed from the storerooms below, ringing through the stones, so frightening he retreated.

'Father, I am not staying here.'

'I agree with that.' The priest struggled to his feet and they fled from Midnight Tower. Ralph insisted that Father Aylred return with him to his own chamber. They stopped at the kitchen where a sleepy-eyed pot boy cut chunks from a flitch of bacon for them and laid the meat on a platter. He then sliced some of the bread Ralph helped him lower from where it was kept in wire baskets hanging from the rafters, well away from the mice and vermin which plagued the castle kitchens.

'Strange, isn't it?' Father Aylred smiled as they climbed the steps back to Ralph's chamber. 'After such encounters I always feel the same, hungry and weak.'

Once inside, Ralph locked the door. He stared carefully around. When they'd left, he hadn't locked the chamber. He quietly vowed never to do that again even though nothing had been disturbed. He cut up the bacon and bread and shared them out, re-filling their wine cups. The old Franciscan had now recovered his poise.

'I first discovered such horrors the night Phoebe died,' he explained. 'At first I thought it was my own imaginings but, each evening, around midnight, I'd return, determined to prove that I am not fey-witted. Each time it grows worse.'

'Hasn't anyone else noticed?'

'Whispers have begun, gossip, chatter. As you know, Ralph, Midnight Tower is not a favoured place during the hours of darkness.'

'Father, you call yourself a simple priest yet what do you think is really happening?'

'As I have said, evil has taken up camp at Ravenscroft. It is linked, like a chain, to the evil which flourished here before.'

'What can be done?'

'I'll say a Mass there, offer it up for the repose of souls and write to the local bishop. More importantly, we must unmask this evil and confront it.' Father Aylred scratched his greying hair. 'But that's easier said than done.' He put his cup down, got to his feet and patted Ralph on the shoulder. 'Lock the door, say your prayers and be careful.'

Ralph let him out then sat for a while at his table, listening to the faint sounds of the castle. It was well past midnight. Grief over Beatrice welled up within him.

'I wish you were here.' He spoke softly into the darkness. 'I wish I could see you just one more time. If I could, I would tell you how much I love you. Death has not changed that. I will love you for as long as I live and beyond.'

He closed his eyes, summoning up Beatrice's face. He didn't know whether it was imagination but he grew warmer, calmer. He opened his eyes quickly. He was almost sure she was here, like the candle flame burning so brightly. He crossed himself, tugged off his boots and lay down on the bed. Beatrice was gone but her murder had to be avenged, he thought as his mind slipped in and out of sleep, but who was the killer? And who had seen him go into Devil's Spinney this morning?

Ralph woke heavy-eyed next morning. He stripped, shaved and washed in the ice-cold water brought up from the butts outside the tower. He went across to the chapel and arrived just in time for the early morning Mass. Afterwards he found Beardsmore and six archers waiting for him in the great hall, breaking their fast. The sergeant-at-arms gestured at the platter of cheese and bread.

'Eat quickly,' he urged. 'We have business in Maldon. I don't want any whispers creeping out.'

Ralph sat opposite the sergeant-at-arms and quaffed the ale but left the cheese and bread as his stomach felt unsettled.

Beardsmore looked at him closely. 'What do you think of last night, sir?' he asked as the archers left to prepare their mounts.

Ralph held the soldier's gaze. He trusted Father Aylred. Could he trust this man?

'We have a common bond,' Beardsmore insisted. 'We have both lost someone we love and we both know it was murder.'

Ralph stretched his hand out. Beardsmore looked surprised but clasped it.

'I trust you, sir,' Ralph said quietly, 'though God knows why. When we have finished this business in Maldon, I must have words with you.'

An hour later they clattered into the village. The high street was fairly deserted. Stalls and booths had not been set up. Peasants and cottagers were still making their way out to the fields. They stopped and looked surly-eyed at the mailed men from the castle. The Pot of Thyme was shuttered and closed. Beardsmore kicked at the door until a haggard-faced serving girl answered.

'What do you want?' Her tone was surly.

Beardsmore shoved her aside and walked in. He dug into his pouch, took out Sir John's writ and, finding a nail in one of the supporting posts, pushed the commission onto it.

'Right!' He started kicking away stools and tables. 'Where's the taverner?'

'I'm here, Beardsmore.' A small, grey-faced man with greasy black hair stepped out of the scullery behind the wine vats. He wiped dirty fingers on a leather apron and stood, legs apart, as if to show he was not frightened of this show of force. 'What do you want?'

Beardsmore pointed to the commission.

'I can't read but I can see the seal.' The taverner's heavy-lidded glance moved to Ralph. 'You're here about Goodman Winthrop, aren't you?'

'You were always quick of wit, Master Taylis,' Beardsmore replied. 'Goodman Winthrop was a tax collector and the King's official. He was found stabbed, his corpse left on the high road.' He pointed to the hour candle. 'Before noon he will be buried in the castle cemetery.'

'Quite a few deaths in the castle,' the taverner remarked. Ralph would have stepped forward but Beardsmore held him back.

'What happens in the castle, Master Taylis, is none of your business. However, it is our business what happens in your tavern.'

'Goodman Winthrop wasn't killed here.'

'He was seen drinking here. We also have it on good report that he left with a wench. I want to speak to her.'

'I don't know who she is. Some wandering whore who stopped in the village.'

'If that's the way you wish to dance, Master Taverner,' Beardsmore snapped, 'then dance you will!'

He drew his two-handed sword and walked towards the

taverner who quickly stepped back. Ralph was too surprised to intervene. The sword came up in one great cutting arc and sliced down into the wooden wine vat. It splintered and cracked, its contents splashing out.

'For the love of God!' Taylis roared. His hand went to the knife beneath his apron.

One of the archers brought up his arbalest and released the bolt which whistled above the taverner's head to bury itself deep in the plaster.

'That's good burgundy!' Taylis bellowed. 'It cost seven pounds!'

'Before I'm finished it's going to cost you more.'

'You can't!'

Beardsmore was already stepping forward, sword level, ready to strike at a second vat. 'Goodman Winthrop,' he declared, 'was a royal official. He drank in this tavern. He left here with a wench. He was murdered. To refuse to help the Crown apprehend his assassins is treason.' He spread his feet, balancing his sword. 'When you are sent to Newgate in London to stand trial before the King's Bench, Master Taylis, who will care about your vats of wine? They'll be Crown property anyway.' The sword came up.

'No!' Taylis shrieked. 'Eleanora!'

'Eleanora? Never heard of her.' Beardsmore raised his sword higher.

'Stay there!' Taylis ran back into the scullery.

They heard shouts and screams. Taylis came back grasping a young, greasy-haired slattern by the shoulder. She was dressed in a dark-brown smock which was two sizes too short for her and emphasised her swelling breasts and broad hips. One of the archers whistled provocatively. The girl turned and spat in Taylis's face but the taverner forced her to her knees in front of Beardsmore. The sergeant-at-arms crouched down, jabbed his finger under her chin and lifted her head.

'You're a buxom wench, Eleanora. How would you like to visit the castle? There are dungeons beneath the moat, full of rats, they are. Worse than you'll ever find at the Pot of Thyme.' He grinned at the taverner. 'Of course some of the lads here can keep you company but not for long. You'll stand trial before Sir John Grasse. He will prove that you had a hand in Winthrop's death. The least you can expect is to hang, which takes some time – the rope tightens round your neck like a cord round a sack, tighter and tighter until you've got no breath left.'

The girl's face went slack with fear.

'Then again,' Beardsmore went on 'you might have to face the full rigours of treason. If that happens, you could be hanged and then dismembered. No, no, I'm wrong.' He teasingly tapped his head. 'You're a woman, you could burn.'

'I didn't do anything,' Eleanora whimpered.

'But you drank with him, yes?'

The girl nodded.

'And you left the tavern with him?'

Again a nod.

'And what happened then?'

'He wanted me to go back to the castle that night. So I left him and ran back here.'

'Is that true, Master Taverner?'

Taylis gazed back, bleak-eyed.

'You see, Eleanora,' said Beardsmore. 'That's what happens when you lie, particularly about treason. No one wants to get involved. Now, what I'll do is arrest the whole tavern, everyone who was here that night, including Master Taylis. I'll ask them all one question: did you come back.'

Taylis regained his wits. 'Of course she did.'

'And then what did she do?' Beardsmore didn't wait for an answer but got to his feet, dragging the girl with him. 'Eleanora, I am placing you under arrest.'

The girl threw herself about but the archers seized her, handling her roughly. Ralph shouted that they were not to abuse her. The archers looked at Beardsmore who nodded.

'Master Taylis, I shall return.' Beardsmore raised his voice. 'I do hope no one leaves. If I can't find certain people because they've suddenly discovered they have business in Chelmsford or Colchester, I'll know they are my suspects.'

They bundled Eleanora out of the tavern. One of the archers put her up on his horse. The cavalcade mounted and left, going back along the high street. Ralph felt sorry for the girl but knew that Beardsmore was correct. She had probably been the lure, a ploy to take Goodman Winthrop out into the dark to be killed, and the law would have its way.

He did not like what he saw as their horses trotted up the cobbled high street. Rumours were rife about how castles had been attacked elsewhere in Essex and Kent, royal officials wounded, even murdered. Ralph realised that Sir John Grasse had made a serious mistake: the people of Maldon were plotting rebellion. He could tell that from the hateful looks, the way women turned away, slamming doors and shutters. And as they left the village, a clod of earth narrowly missed Ralph's head.

'There'll be trouble before long,' said Beardsmore grimly.

Ralph pulled his horse back so as to protect Eleanora from the salacious jibes and pokes of the escorting archers. Once they were clear of the town, Beardsmore reined in, dismounted and dragged Eleanora from the saddle. He cut her bonds and took her away from the rest, indicating that Ralph should join them. They walked along the trackway and stopped under a sycamore tree.

'Look, mistress,' Beardsmore said kindly, 'I no more wish to see you hang than I would my own sister.'

The tavern wench stared dourly back. 'What do you want?' she asked, pawing at her dusty skirt.

'Not what you think,' Beardsmore said drily. 'But I can protect you. I do not want to see your pretty neck twisted. I want to arrest the nimble jacks who killed Goodman Winthrop. I'll tell you what will really happen. You'll be taken to the castle, Sir John will keep you until the royal commissioners arrive. Then the merry jig will begin. They won't care about who you are or where you are from. They will regard you as a hungry mastiff would a piece of meat.'

Eleanora's courage deserted her, her shoulders sagged

and she muttered, 'I can name them. And I can also tell you why.'

'Why what?' Beardsmore asked, glancing in puzzlement at Ralph.

'I hate the castle,' she replied.

Beardsmore was growing impatient. 'Woman, what are you talking about?'

Ralph looked back down the trackway. The archers were laughing and talking among themselves. It was turning into a dull grey afternoon. The countryside lay quiet, even the birds had ceased their chirping. Up ahead he could see the towers and crenellated walls of Ravenscroft. He became distracted; his father had once told him how he could judge the date of a hedge by the number and different species of trees it contained. If that was the case, this must be the same hedge Cerdic had passed when he had fled from the battle at Blackwater. Ralph shook himself from his reverie.

'I was sweet on Fulk,' Eleanora was saying. 'He's the miller's son.'

Beardsmore nodded. 'He has disappeared, hasn't he?'

'It's not that,' Eleanora replied. She scratched at the sweat on her neck with blackened nails and glanced sideways at Ralph. 'We saw murder, we did.'

Beardsmore grasped her by the shoulder. 'What murder?'

'The castle wench, Phoebe. We were in Devil's Spinney.' Eleanora now smiled slyly as if she sensed the tables were turned. 'Me and Fulk, lying there in the long grass, hidden in the dusk. Fulk became afeared; he raised himself up. "Hush," he whispered. "Someone's coming!" I thought he was teasing but he grabbed me by the arms.' She grinned. 'I couldn't get up because my shift was all awry so we lay and watched. A dark shape came through the trees. He was carrying a bundle, cords wrapped round it. He put the bundle down.'

'How do you know it was a man?' Beardsmore interrupted.

'I don't. Whoever it was was dressed like a monk, in a long robe and cowl. Fulk said the figure wore a mask. Anyway, the cords were cut, the bundle unrolled. Fulk whispered it was the corpse of a young woman.'

'And then?' Beardsmore asked, still gripping her shoulders.

'Fulk said he wanted to see who it was. He went over to the edge of the spinney and watched this mysterious intruder go back towards the castle.'

'Didn't you think of raising the alarm?' Ralph asked.

'Why should we? Fulk was frightened that we'd get the blame.'

'Did he see who it was?'

'He thought he knew but he wasn't certain and wouldn't answer my questions. The following evening Fulk's father came to the tavern. He said his son had left early for Ravenscroft and had not returned.' Eleanora's eyes became hard. 'That's why I hate the castle, and so do the townspeople. We heard about Phoebe, Fulk went to the castle and then he disappeared.'

'I've heard enough.' Beardsmore growled and, pushing the girl before him, they went back to their horses.

Chapter 3

Ralph attended Sir John Grasse's council meeting held that afternoon in the castle solar. Eleanora had been confined to one of the dungeons in Bowyer Tower with a guard placed outside. Sir John, his wife Lady Anne, Theobald Vavasour, Father Aylred, Adam and Marisa, Beardsmore and himself gathered round the wooden, oval table in the Constable's private quarters. Lady Anne tried to lighten the atmosphere, serving goblets of chilled white wine and small trays of sweetmeats. They all listened as Beardsmore delivered his report. Before Sir John could respond, Father Aylred, agitated and anxious, sprang to his feet. He was unshaven, eyes red-rimmed; Ralph secretly wondered if the hideous events of the previous night had disturbed his wits.

'I am a priest, Sir John, dedicated to the care of souls. I do believe something very wicked has entered this castle.'

'Yes, yes,' Sir John interrupted impatiently. 'Of that we are certain. Phoebe's death, the attack on Master Ralph, the disappearance of Fulk. The facts speak for themselves.'

'No, no, I talk of other things,' the priest said hurriedly. 'Ralph and I have been to Midnight Tower.'

'Ah, yes. You told me about that. The tower has always had an evil reputation.'

'But the phantasms, the phenomena!' the priest cried, rubbing the side of his face.

'Father.' Ralph got up, came round and gently eased him back into his chair. 'The evil we face is of human origin, and it is human wit and good counselling that will reveal the truth.'

The priest calmed down and Ralph returned to his chair.

'Sir John, if I may speak?'

The Constable nodded.

'We have had a number of strange occurrences here,' Ralph began, 'but logic and reason can untangle any mystery.'

The others stared owlishly at him, except Adam, who winked mischievously.

'Ever the clerk, eh, Ralph?'

'Yes, Adam, ever the clerk. We know Phoebe was alive last Monday afternoon. We have established that her corpse was found in Devil's Spinney the following Tuesday, yes?'

They all agreed.

'We know that the wench Eleanora and her young lover Fulk were in those woods when Phoebe's corpse was taken there. Accordingly, Phoebe must have been killed some time late on Monday afternoon, here in the castle; her corpse was wrapped in a sheet, bound with cords and taken out to Devil's Spinney by her assassin.'

'But that's impossible!' Beardsmore cried. 'I was on guard duty at the barbican. No one passed me carrying such a bundle: I would have seen it. We have both checked the postern gate. It has not been opened for years.'

'Sir John,' said Ralph, 'is there a secret passageway out of this castle?'

The Constable shook his head. 'If there was, Ralph, I'd know. And how can there be? The moat is deep, any passageway would have to go under it so it's nigh impossible.'

'Why?' Marisa asked.

'Because,' Adam replied languidly, 'the water would seep through any man-made structure and flood the tunnel.'

Ralph sipped his wine and took another piece of marchpane from the plate. 'Nonetheless, what I have said is true. How the assassin left carrying the corpse must, for the time being, remain a mystery.' He pulled a face. 'So, my next question is, what were we all doing that Monday afternoon?'

'I was in my chamber,' Theobald answered quickly. 'I never left there, not till the bell rang for supper. I was studying the innards of a rat.' There were cries of disgust. 'I read in a treatise from Italy,' he explained, 'that the innards of a rat, dried and ground to powder, are a veritable cure for certain skin diseases.'

'Did anyone visit you there?' Sir John asked.

The physician shook his head.

'No one would dare go there,' Lady Anne said tartly. 'Such smells and odours!'

The others also gave an account of themselves. Few could

114

offer any witnesses except Adam who had been going through the list of stores in the castle with Marisa. 'We were there all afternoon,' he concluded.

'And I can vouch for that,' Sir John declared. 'I heard your voice, and Marisa's. As for myself, I dined here in the hall then I went for a sleep.'

'Whilst I,' Lady Anne pointed to the spinning wheel near the window seat, 'read a little and worked on the wheel. You came over, Father. You asked if you could borrow some candlesticks for the altar.'

The priest picked at a stain on his robe. 'True, I was in my chapel, cleaning the sacred vessels.' He flailed his hands in despair. 'Master Ralph, what is the use of all this?'

'And you?' Ralph asked the sergeant-at-arms.

'I dined with Sir John,' Beardsmore replied. 'And then I did my guard duty. I stayed with the other lads in the barbican.'

Ralph ran his thumbnail round his lips. 'Sir John, we do have one loose thread: Fulk the miller's son. From what Eleanora has told us, Fulk may have recognised the person who carried Phoebe's corpse into the spinney. He must have come to the castle and demanded to see someone.'

'That could be very easily established. Wait there.' Beardsmore hurriedly left the solar, clattering down the stairs.

Sir John took advantage of the break to order the wine cups to be refilled. He loudly speculated on what they should do with their new prisoner. 'There is no doubt,' he announced, eager to assert his authority, 'that the tavern slattern had a hand in Goodman Winthrop's death. But what can we do? Put her to the torture? We have enough discontent in Maldon.'

'Keep her safe,' Ralph replied. 'Wait for the commissioners to arrive from London. Let them take responsibility.'

Sir John nodded. 'Adam, when this is finished, go down to Maldon, tell the taverner Taylis that Eleanora will be kept safe and secure. We will not harm a hair on her head. I just wish this business was finished.' He looked at Aylred. 'Father, I regret my sharp words earlier. Perhaps you could say a Mass in Midnight Tower and give the place a blessing.'

The priest agreed.

Ralph was studying Theobald, who appeared agitated. Of all the people present, he was the most solitary and most secretive. Ralph glanced at Adam and Marisa sitting hand in hand. Marisa was staring adoringly at her husband. Ralph felt a tug at his heart and tried to curb his envy at their closeness. They heard footsteps and Beardsmore strode back into the chamber.

'I've made inquiries among the guards.' He shook his head. 'So many people come in and out of the castle, Sir John. One guard thinks he may have seen Fulk coming here early on Tuesday morning but Phoebe's corpse had yet to be discovered. No one was stopped or challenged.'

Sir John put his cup down. 'We've done what we can.'

Ralph was angry and disappointed at the lack of new information the meeting had produced. 'There's an assassin in the castle.' he said heatedly. 'He or she killed without mercy. The assassin could well be in this chamber.' He go to his feet, kicking the chair back. 'I would warn you all to be most careful.'

He was halfway across the bailey when Beardsmore caught up with him.

'Master Ralph, do you trust me?'

'Why do you ask?'

'If the killer is in this castle then he or she must be someone in authority.'

'What makes you say that?'

'Oh, clerk, look around. Can you imagine any of the archers or the men-at-arms, the cooks, the scullions, the servants taking such pains over the disposing of poor Phoebe's corpse? She wasn't killed in some kitchen fight or because an archer wanted to ruffle her skirts. She was killed for something else. Something she saw or heard. Whoever it was managed to find a secret way out with the corpse. Everyone at that meeting will go back to their chambers and start to think.'

'And you don't want the finger of suspicion pointed at you.'

'No, I don't.' Beardsmore tightened his war belt. 'I have to check certain matters. Meet me at the barbican within the hour.' The sergeant-at-arms walked away.

Ralph remembered Eleanora and crossed to Bowyer Tower. He opened the door and went down the steps. The dungeons consisted of three cells off a passageway built into the base of the tower. They were well-swept and clean, usually reserved for stores. Two archers now sat across the passage playing dice, a jug of ale and some beakers on the ground beside them.

Pitch torches flickered in the darkness. From the middle cell came the sound of crooning.

'She's happy enough,' one of the archers declared as Ralph squatted beside him. The fellow wiped his nose on the back of his hand. 'More comfortable than we are.'

'And you don't trouble her?'

The archer shook his head. 'Master Beardsmore was most insistent. She's to be kept warm and plump for the royal commissioners.'

'I would like to speak to her.'

The archer pocketed his dice, got to his feet and took a key from a hook in the wall. He opened the door and ushered Ralph in.

Eleanora was comfortable enough; the cell was clean, fresh grass had been cut and strewn on the floor. She had a cot bed with a bolster and blankets, a table, stool, a shelf for cups and jugs; even a small crucifix hung from one of the window bars high in the wall. The tavern wench was sitting in the corner, knees up, making a doll out of straw she had pulled from the mattress.

'You are well, Mistress?'

'I would prefer to be back at the Pot of Thyme, sitting on a customer's knee and sharing a tankard of ale. But I'm well looked after. I've had bread, roast goose.' She pointed to a jug on the table. 'And some watery ale. The old priest came down to see me but he was more nervous than I am.'

'Do you think Fulk saw Phoebe's murderer?'

'I think he did but Fulk was tight-lipped. I asked him but

he just stared at me in that strange way of his. You know, out of the corner of his eye, just like his father does when he makes a profit with that golden thumb of his.'

'So why do you think Fulk came back to the castle?'

Eleanora's eyes shifted.

'Why should he come back?' Ralph persisted. He got up and moved towards her. 'Did he tell you?'

Again a flicker of the eyes.

'Come on, did he? Why should Fulk the miller's son be interested in a murderer? He came here to extort money, didn't he? He didn't return, so you put it about in the Pot of Thyme tavern that he was on some innocent errand to the castle and didn't come back.'

'I will tell all,' Eleanora declared defiantly, 'when the King's men come. I wish to be alone. Sir John Grasse promised I wouldn't be troubled.'

Ralph left the dungeon. He walked up into the keep looking for Father Aylred but the chapel was empty. He stayed for a while, kneeling in the entrance to the rood screen, staring up at the cross.

'I am not a prayerful man,' he murmured. 'In fact, I don't know what I am. But, Lord, I am very frightened. And I miss Beatrice.'

Ralph closed his eyes. In a week his whole life had been shattered, like the wine vat Beardsmore had sliced in the Pot of Thyme tavern. He made himself more comfortable, with his back to the rood screen, and stared up at the corbels on the roof. He noticed the gargoyle, a grinning jester with his fingers in his mouth. In his imagination the face became that of the killer, quietly mocking him from the shadows. Ralph looked away. He had been so engrossed in trying to find out who the killer was, how these deaths and attacks had occurred, he had not asked why the peaceable life of this castle had abruptly changed. True, there was unrest in the countryside but the attacks, apart from that on Phoebe, had been directed at him. Ralph wondered what Beatrice would have thought and said. She had a sharp mind. If only she was here, sitting next to him.

The sunlight was now streaming through the window, the dust motes dancing, and he wondered if they were angels. He felt warm and relaxed.

He heard a sound down the church and whirled round, peering through the rood screen, then he remembered locking and barring the door behind him. He got to his feet and stared round the little sanctuary. The cross on the altar was dazzling in the light of the sun. He felt alert but not distraught, as if he had woken from a refreshing sleep. He looked at the gleaming cross.

'The treasure,' he murmured. He knelt on the prie-dieu, eyes fixed on that cross. 'The only thing anyone else would want is Brythnoth's cross but I haven't got it yet.'

He recalled the May Day celebrations, the castle officers assembled on the green. Ralph repressed a shiver and bowed his head. He had thought of this before, and now he was forced to accept it: his boasting had caused all this. Someone at that meal had decided to intervene, someone who had been following his search most closely. His chamber was often unlocked, with manuscripts left on the table. Never once had he suspected that someone would take up the hunt with him.

Ralph broke out in a sweat. He had to face the truth. He was supposed to have been on the parapet walk. He was supposed to have died in Devil's Spinney. And Phoebe? She had been a pert-faced, sharp-tongued wench with a nose for mischief and an ear for other people's conversations. She must have seen or heard something and been brutally silenced. But how had her corpse been taken out of the castle? Ralph remembered Beardsmore, crossed himself and almost fled from the church. His mind was all a jumble as guilt pricked at his grief. He strode across the castle bailey. Beardsmore was waiting for him on the steps of the barbican guardhouse.

'Are you well, Master Ralph? You look pale.'

Ralph grasped him by the elbow and took him out on the drawbridge.

'I know why Beatrice died,' he said in a rush. 'Because of Brythnoth's treasure – you know, from chatter, my interest in it. They think I am close to finding the cross.'

'They?'

'Whoever killed Beatrice and attacked me in Devil's Spinney. That's why Phoebe died, she saw or heard something.' He led Beardsmore even further away, out of the shadows into the full sunlight. 'The killer must be one of the castle council, that's why Fulk came here. He was going to blackmail him or her. He wanted silver for his silence.'

'But where's Fulk now?'

Ralph waved his hands. 'I don't know. Master Beardsmore, I trust you completely. You are the only one I do trust. Anyway, you asked me to meet you here. What do you propose?'

'A walk round the moat, Master Ralph.' He moved to the left, walking through the long grass which fringed the edge of the moat. 'Keep behind me,' he ordered. 'Study the ground, look for anything untoward. A piece of cloth, dried blood. Anything that shouldn't be there.'

Pinching his nostrils against the rank smell from the slimy water, Ralph obeyed. He understood Beardsmore's logic. If Phoebe's corpse had not been carried through the barbican or the rusting postern gate, some other route must have been taken. Now and again he'd stop and stare over the heathland towards Devil's Spinney. A merlin hovered, wings whirling, above the trees, searching for prey. Butterflies and bees moved among the clusters of wild flowers. The click of grasshoppers broke the silence. A sentry noticed them and shouted out some greeting. Beardsmore simply raised his hand in acknowledgement.

They went along the side of the castle, then round the back. Ralph rarely came here. To the north stretched moorland dotted by copses of trees; against the blue sky curled the odd plume of grey smoke from a woodcutter's or charcoal-burner's cottage. In the centre of the rear wall rose the Salt Tower. The masonry was crumbling, some had fallen into the moat. Beardsmore stopped before this, narrowing his eyes.

'It's disused now,' he said. 'The steps are not too safe.'

Ralph looked up at the shuttered windows though Beardsmore was more interested in the moat. The water was shallower here and fallen masonry from the Salt Tower had created a makeshift causeway across the moat. On the far side against the wall a bank of mud had formed.

'I wonder,' Beardsmore murmured. 'Look at the tower. What do you see?'

'Windows on the higher floors, a window door lower down.'

'In former times it was used to bring stores in. A way of victualling the castle without using the barbican.' Beardsmore warily made his way through the reeds and, splashing and slipping, ran across the makeshift causeway to the muddy bank beneath the Salt Tower. He had to hold himself against the wall, for it was no more than a narrow ledge. He eased himself down and studied the ground. With a cry of triumph he drew his dagger, dug at the mud and held up a ring which flashed in the sunlight.

'I knew it!' he declared. 'This is how they took Phoebe's corpse out.'

Re-sheathing his dagger and grasping the ring, Beardsmore splashed back across the moat and showed Ralph what he had found. The ring was one of those sold at many fairs or market booths.

'Phoebe bought this from a chapman who came here just after the feast of the Purification. She was very proud of it.' The sergeant scratched his coarse, cropped hair and stared back at the Salt Tower. 'She must have been lured into the tower, beaten and strangled, and then her corpse, wrapped and tied with cords, was lowered from that door. The assassin then let himself down, picked up the corpse and hurried into Devil's Spinney. Remember, Eleanora said it was dark. The corpse was placed in the spinney and the assassin re-entered the castle, probably by the same route.' He gripped Ralph's arm. 'You know I speak the truth.'

'You speak the truth, Master Beardsmore.' Ralph smiled. 'The castle walls are undefended. This is a lonely part, no one would notice. If Eleanora and Fulk had not been in the spinney, no one would have been the wiser.' Ralph walked towards the moat. 'We should tell Sir John about this. If the castle was ever attacked—' He heard a sound; a creak, as if a shutter was opening, followed by a whirring noise. He looked back over his shoulder and stared in horror.

Beardsmore was swaying on his feet, hands out, eyes rolled up at the crossbow bolt which had taken him dead centre in the forehead. Ralph ran towards him. Beardsmore sighed and fell into his arms. Ralph laid him down on the grass. His eyelids fluttered; he coughed blood, jerked and lay still, his hand still holding Phoebe's ring. Ralph stretched across to take it. The action saved his life; a crossbow bolt skimmed the air above him. Ralph looked up at the Salt Tower. One of the windows at the top was open.

He stared around. What could he do? There was no cover. The next bolt skimmed over his shoulder. Too fast, Ralph thought, the hidden archer must have more than one crossbow primed. He considered using Beardsmore's corpse as a shield but it would still leave him exposed. He flinched as a bolt struck just near his knee. He pushed Beardsmore's corpse aside and fled at an angle to the edge of the moat and dived in. He remembered to keep his mouth closed but opened his eyes. The water was light green, about six feet deep; thick weeds impeded his progress. Ralph pushed them aside. If he could move further down the moat and get out, he'd be safe. The weeds, however, clutched at him and panic gripped him. His chest was hurting; his eyes stinging. He could not swim for much longer; he had to get out. He moved some weeds aside and opened his mouth in a silent scream as a corpse reached up to greet him, face liverish, eyes staring, tendrils of hair moving in the water. Ralph pushed the body away and reached the bank. The rushes here afforded some protection. He lay against the mud, gasping for breath, and stared back along the bank. He had swum a good few yards but to him it seemed like miles. Beardsmore's corpse lay sprawled on the heathland. From the parapet above, Ralph heard the shouts of sentries – they had spotted Beardsmore's body. Wearily Ralph pulled himself out, covered in mud and slime. He clambered on to the bank and stared back into the moat; no sign of the corpse but he guessed who it was.

'Poor Fulk,' he muttered. 'That's the only reward you earned.'

Despite the pain in his side, Ralph ran along the wall, determined to reach the barbican. His eyes stung and the moat water had coated his mouth. He had hardly turned the corner when Adam came running out, Marisa behind him, her hair flying. Ralph collapsed into his friends' arms.

'Beardsmore's dead!' he gasped. 'The Salt Tower. There's a corpse in the moat – Fulk's. Father Aylred is right: the Devil has set up camp at Ravenscroft!'

Chapter 4

Ralph stared down at the two corpses laid out in their makeshift coffins on trestles beneath the steps leading up to the keep. Theobald Vavasour had removed the crossbow quarrel from Beardsmore's head and dressed the wound. Ralph felt a deep sadness. This young soldier, so full of life and energy, so determined to bring the killer of his lover to justice, now nothing more than a heap of dead flesh. In the coffin next to him lay the body of young Fulk, his face a whitish-blue. Despite all the efforts of the physician, his eyes would not remain closed; his face was bloated, his corpse soggy with water. Father Aylred had given both the last rites but it was obvious the priest was at the end of his tether. He forgot words and his hands shook so much that Ralph had to help him administer the holy oils. Sir John eventually sent him back to his chamber to rest then despatched Theobald to make sure he was all right.

Sir John scuffed the grass with his boot. 'Adam, when you go down to Maldon, you'd best take Fulk's corpse with you.'

'How was he killed?' Adam asked.

Ralph turned the sodden corpse over, displaying the blood-clotted hair. 'A blow to the back of the head.'

'And you, Ralph, are you all right?'

'I've washed and changed yet again.' Ralph tried to put a brave face on it. 'I feel a little queasy from the moat water I've drunk but otherwise I'll survive.' He drew closer to them. 'Sir John, the assassin killed Beardsmore but he was trying to kill me. It should be easy to find out where everyone was.'

'I've done so already,' the Constable replied. 'Adam here helped me. Father Aylred was in the chapel, or claims he was. He had smashed an offertory cruet and was clearing up the mess.'

'But I left the chapel just before meeting Beardsmore,' said Ralph. 'I never saw him there.'

'That's where he claims he was and I've seen the broken glass.'

'And Theobald?'

'In his chamber, poring over a book on alchemy.'

Ralph held his gaze.

'I know. I know,' Sir John murmured. 'I was walking round the castle talking to this person and that. Lady Anne was her chamber.'

'And you, Adam?'

His friend stretched out his hands, the fingers covered ink. 'I was in the chancery office, Marisa was there wi me. If you go up there now you'll find the documents a manuscripts littering my table. I spilled some ink when the alarm was raised.'

'That was one of the guards,' Sir John informed them. 'He was sunning himself and, by chance, looked over the wall. Beardsmore was down. He thought your assailant was outside the castle.'

'Well,' Adam sighed, 'at least we know Fulk did come here.'

Ralph walked away from the coffins. 'I suspect that the person Fulk met told him to leave.' He smacked the heel of his hand against his forehead. 'No, no, he didn't do that! Sir John, Adam, come with me!'

They walked round the keep, through the orchard and across the overgrown garden to the Salt Tower. A deserted, derelict place. Brambles and gorse sprouted through the travelled path stretching up to the walls of the tower, almost blocking the door leading into it. They pushed through the friars which caught at their leggings and boots.

Ralph put a hand to the door and it swung open. 'It should be locked!' Sir John exclaimed. 'The tower is unsafe.'

Ralph crouched down and peered at the lock. 'It's been forced. The lock is rusty and so is the catch. It wouldn't take much force.'

Inside, it smelled of mildew and damp. Great cobwebs stretched like nets in the corners. The stairwell was dirty, the steps up crumbling and covered in dust. Ralph looked for any mark or sign.

'Someone has been here, the dust has been disturbed.'

'Is it safe?' Adam asked.

'We'll find out.'

Ralph began to climb. He reached the first landing and pushed open the door to a chamber. At the far end was the broad shuttered window door he had glimpsed on the other side of the moat, about four feet high. The chamber itself was shabby and grim. The plaster had fallen off the wall and the room stank of the rotten rushes left lying there. He walked across, lifted the bar to the shutters and swung them open welcoming the rush of clean air. Below him the moat glinted. Ralph stared across the heathland.

'I think this is where the assassin brought Phoebe's corpse wrapped in a canvas sheet. He lowered it on to the muddy bank below, crossed the moat, left the corpse in Devil's Spinney and returned by the same route. It was quite easily done.' He peered down. 'He probably used a pole or spear to close the door behind him when he was on the bank. He'd leave the spear thrust into the mud until he returned and use it to open the shutters again. Look at the walls, Sir John, there are enough gaps and rents; it would be as easy as climbing a ladder.'

'And the same for Fulk?' Adam asked.

'I suspect so. The assassin probably lured the young man here with the prospect of silver and gold.' Ralph pulled the shutter closed. 'A swift blow to the head and again he'd lower the corpse, throw it into the moat and climb back.'

'Your troubles haven't dimmed your wits,' Adam smiled.

'I agree, Sir John.' He stared round the shabby room. 'The

place has seen terrible murders.' He walked round, staring at the floor.

'I don't think you'll find anything,' said Ralph. 'Our killer is too sly and cunning for that.'

'But wouldn't all this be noticed?' Sir John snapped, shuffling his feet, plucking at his war belt in his agitation. His happy, humdrum existence had been shattered by bloody murder and he knew he would face harsh questioning from the King's men when they arrived.

Ralph shook his head. 'This is a deserted part of the castle. Until yesterday no guards walked the parapet except some sleepy-eyed sentry, and he'd make himself as comfortable as possible. No, the killer had it all his own way.' Ralph gestured at the window door. 'I'd advise you to have those shutters barred and padlocked. If the castle is ever attacked, that's our weakest point.' He walked towards the door.

'Where to now?' Adam asked.

Ralph didn't answer, more intent on climbing the spiral staircase, studying each step as he went. The chamber at the top had no door. He walked in and went across to the two windows, one facing him, the other to the side. The room was similar to the one he had left, dirty and squalid. The bars on the shutter lifted easily and he noticed that the hinges had been recently oiled. He opened one shutter and stared down at the spot where he and Beardsmore had been standing. Then he moved across to the shutter in the right wall of this box-like chamber. He opened it and looked out on a good view of the moat right along the castle wall.

'This is where Beardsmore's assassin stood,' he declared. 'He fired first from the facing window and, when I fled, moved across to the side which provides a view from the flank of the tower.'

Sir John looked through both windows, the wind whipping his white hair, making his eyes water.

'I've sent a sentry out.' He turned and leaned against the wall. 'Including the quarrel which killed Beardsmore, at least five crossbow bolts were loosed.'

Ralph stared out of the window. He had liked Beardsmore and felt guilty at the suspicions of him he had nursed earlier, but at the same time the sergeant-at-arms' death seemed to have calmed his grief for Beatrice. Instead he felt an implacable desire to bring her killer to justice. He had seen a man hang once and had hated it, but he quietly conceded that he'd stand and enjoy this assassin have the life throttled out of him! Someone in this castle had watched him meet Beardsmore at the gatehouse and walk round the moat; he'd feared that Beardsmore would either find out how Phoebe's corpse was removed or discover the whereabouts of poor Fulk's corpse.

'Yes, that's it!' he exclaimed.

'What is?' Adam asked.

'The assassin meant to kill both Beardsmore and myself.'

'Why?' Sir John asked.

'I'm not sure,' Ralph replied cautiously. 'But I tell you, Sir John, this castle should be put on a war footing. Every tower, every gateway should have a sentry not only to guard the approaches but to watch who goes where. We should also be very careful about being alone and what we eat or drink.'

'Sir John Grasse! Sir John Grasse!' a voice bellowed from the bottom of the staircase.

'Oh Lord save us! What now?'

'Sir John, followed by his two clerks, clambered down the stairs. The captain of the guard was there, helmet under his arm.

'Sir John, it's the prisoner, the woman Eleanora.'

'Oh, don't say she's escaped.'

'No, sir, she's dead!'

They ran through the overgrown garden and bailey, across the green to Bowyer Tower. The door to the cell was open. Eleanora was sprawled on the floor, mouth gaping, eyes staring; her body was twisted like a piece of cloth, wrung and tossed aside. Father Aylred was sitting on the bed rocking gently backwards and forwards, singing under his breath. Theobald knelt by the corpse. He shook his head as Sir John came in.

'Dead, Sir John. Poisoned.'

'What?' Sir John turned to the captain of the guard.

'Sir, she ate what we ate and drank!'

Ralph crossed to the little table where a platter lay containing the remains of some food.

'I've tested those already,' Theobald said. 'Indeed, when I came in two rats were finishing it off and they seemed none the worse.'

'There are poisons enough in the castle,' Sir John remarked.

'Used to destroy vermin.' He looked at Theobald. 'And of course you have a fine collection of elixirs, haven't you?'

Theobald would have retorted heatedly but Ralph intervened.

'What is important,' he said, 'is how the wench died. You say the food is not tainted?'

'Yes!' Theobald snapped.

Ralph turned to the archers standing in the doorway. 'Did any of you come into the cell?'

'We kept well away from her,' one of them replied.

'And no one came down to visit her?'

'No.' The archer shook his head. 'The Constable's orders were quite clear. She was to be kept comfortable and not disturbed. The only time I came in here was to empty that.' The archer pointed to a chamber pot peeping out from beneath the bed. 'I put in some saltpetre to hide the smell. Apart from that, we left her alone.'

'When did she last eat?'

'Oh, about ten of the clock.'

'Three hours ago.' Ralph stared up at the grille in the wall which looked out on to the castle bailey. 'So how did you find her?'

'The corpse was cold,' Theobald interjected. 'She must have been dead for at least two hours.'

'As I said,' the archer replied, 'we left her in peace. I remembered the chamber pot, looked through the bars and saw her lying there.'

'How on earth did this happen?' Sir John demanded.

'Here's a young woman in her cell. The food and drink are not tainted and yet she's found poisoned by some noxious substance.'

Ralph knelt beside the corpse and put his fingers into the half-open mouth. It was slightly warm. He felt along the gums, the cracked teeth. He felt something half-chewed and pulled it out. Keeping it on the end of his finger, he went to the window. He sniffed, rubbed his finger along the wall and poured some water from the jug over his hands.

'What is it?' Sir John demanded.

'I'm no physician or leech, Sir John. But I think I've just examined the last thing she ate. A sweetmeat, marchpane possibly.'

'But she was never given any!' the guard exclaimed.

Ralph stared up at the grille. 'Someone in this castle approached that window. He secured Eleanora's confidence and dropped a piece of marchpane or something through the bars. Eleanora would relish that. More importantly, she must have trusted the person who gave it to her.'

'But who in the castle knew her?' Adam asked.

'I don't know,' Ralph replied wearily. 'I really don't. Sir John, you'd best get the corpse removed.'

Sir John stamped out of the cell, shouting orders. Ralph followed and went back to his own chamber. He unlocked the door and went in. Everything was as he had left it. He sniffed at the jug of wine and examined the cup before going to sit at his table. He pulled across a scrubbed sheet of vellum, opened the inkpot, sharpened a quill and wrote out a list of names. He included his own among them.

'I'm so confused,' he muttered. 'I could even half convince myself that I've done something wrong.'

He studied the names. Any one of them could have been lurking in that tower the night Beatrice died. And Phoebe? A blow to the back of the head. Yes, they could all do that. And what about the attack on him in Devil's Spinney? That would take some strength. He'd been knocked half unconscious and he recalled being dragged through the grass. The Constable was a strong man. So was Adam. But Theobald and Aylred?

'Yes?' he said aloud. 'They would have the strength.'

And the attack on Fulk? He closed his eyes. He could imagine the miller's son being taken to the Salt Tower, up the steps to that shabby chamber. Fulk would be full of himself, eager to get his hands on the silver to buy his silence. A blow to the back of the head would end all that. And this morning, the attack on Beardsmore? Both Theobald and Father Aylred had done military service. Any of the men on the council could load three or four arbalests and fire them. But Eleanora's death? Whom would she trust?

Ralph put his head in his hands. Where could he start? He recalled the arbalest and the number of quarrels that had been loosed. He should check the armoury. Everyone owned a crossbow, his own stood over in the corner of the room, but four, even five? What about Lady Anne? She was a tall, sinewy woman. She was capable and strong enough for

136

these secret attacks and no stranger to a crossbow. Marisa, too, could not be discounted.

Ralph put on his war belt and left his chamber. He first visited the armoury. The archer guarding the stores shook his head and scratched a weather-beaten cheek.

'You can see for yourself, Master Clerk, if you want, though Sir John's already done it. We have the same number of arbalests as we had this time last week. No one has taken either crossbow or bolts.'

'You are sure?'

'As I am that I am talking to you, sir. Even if the Constable himself came and asked for four or five crossbows, questions would be asked.'

Ralph then visited Father Aylred in his chamber above the chapel. Despite his warnings, the door was off the latch, the priest was asleep on his bed, a half-filled wine cup beside him. Next he went in search of Theobald whom he found busy in his chamber. Ralph always marvelled at how untidy the physician's room was. On hooks in the walls hung garish cloths depicting strange symbols which, Theobald had explained, were the signs of the zodiac. An astrolabe stood on a table, dried frogs, toads and rats hung from more hooks. Bottles and jars littered the desk and shelves; manuscripts and documents lay strewn about. The physician was kneeling on the floor sniffing at a jar which gave off a foul odour.

'You should keep your door locked, Master Vavasour.'

The physician didn't even bother to turn round.

'If I am going to die, Master Ralph, I am going to die. Come in.' He got to his feet, wiping his fingers on his dirty robe. 'Do you know, you are the only person who comes in here and never complains about the smell. So, what do you want?'

Ralph stared round the chamber. 'What are these potions and strange odours?'

Theobald sucked on his teeth. 'You are too young to remember the plague, Ralph, the great pestilence. However, in my journeys, I met a Greek who studied at Montpellier and Salerno.' He moved to the window and opened a shutter. 'I lost both my parents, my brothers and my sisters to the plague. All died within a week. I vowed, one day, I'd find a cure.'

'For the pestilence?' Ralph exclaimed. 'Impossible!'

'That's what everyone says, except the Greek. He'd studied with the Arabs and claimed the pestilence was carried by the black rat. Remove the dirt, kill the rats and the pestilence would die with them. He also said something else: that if you took milk, let it go sour then mixed it with dried moss you could produce a powder, odiferous and unpalatable but, give it to a plague victim, and he could be cured.'

'So, why don't you do it?' Ralph teased.

'I have, with varying degress of success. And it set me wondering. Do powders from dead dried things protect the living?'

Ralph moved the astrolabe and sat down on a stool. 'And have you experimented?'

'On sick animals, yes. Sometimes they live, sometimes they die. I have to be careful, that's why I stay at Ravenscroft. It'.

easy for someone to point a finger and shout witch or warlock. Sir John Grasse protects me. I'm no witch.' He pointed to the stark black crucifix pinned to the wall just inside the door. 'I serve the Lord Jesus in my own way. I fashioned that cross myself from some oak I took out of Devil's Spinney. It's a constant reminder to visitors, to reflect before they accuse.'

Ralph studied the little physician. He had always considered Theobald Vavasour a grey man in looks as well as character. Now he regretted his arrogant judgement. Theobald was intent on finding his own treasure, the secrets of alchemy and medicine, as he was Brythnoth's cross.

'But you haven't come here to discuss physic, have you?'

'Yes and no,' Ralph replied.

'The poisoning?'

'The poisoning,' Ralph nodded. 'What would kill so quickly?'

Theobald spread his hands. 'Look at this chamber, Ralph. If you've come to find evidence then put the chains on my wrists and call the guards. I have henbane, foxglove, belladonna, as well as two types of arsenic, red and white. Sometimes I lock my door, sometimes I don't. Anyone could come in here and take something from my jars. Anyone could go down to the castle's stores, too, and find poison for rats and vermin in the corners. Any of the poisons I have mentioned could have killed that young woman,' he snapped his fingers, 'in a few heartbeats.'

'So quickly?'

'Master Clerk, forget the troubadours' tales. Poison in

sufficient quantities will kill speedily.' He sniffed, doffed his skull cap and placed it on the floor beside him. 'And you suspect me?'

'Somebody had the young woman's trust,' Ralph replied.

Theobald sighed. 'I see, and of course everyone trusts a physician, eh, Ralph?' He shook his head. 'I swear on my parents' graves I never spoke to that young woman.'

Ralph studied him.

'I speak the truth,' Theobald said. 'And, do you know, Ralph, I feel calm. I've lived my life.' He shrugged and got to his feet. 'If I have to die then perhaps Ravenscroft is the friendliest place to end my days.'

Ralph thanked him and left.

Down in the castle bailey two of the coffins had been lifted on to a cart to be taken to the village. Beardsmore's was being carried up to the chapel. Sir John had placed a black pall over it. Ralph walked on to the green and paused. It seemed an age since he had sat beside Beatrice on that lovely sunny afternoon before the shadows came racing in. He felt a deep sense of sorrow and found himself walking towards the steps to the parapet walk from which Beatrice had fallen. Two sentries now stood on guard at either end. Ralph stopped in the centre and stared across at Devil's Spinney.

'It's the treasure,' he whispered, the wind catching his words. 'Brythnoth's cross caused all this.'

He thought of his visit to Theobald's room. The cross! The black cross nailed to the wall! Theobald claimed he had fashioned it from an oak in the spinney. Ralph laughed. It was so easy! A child-like solution to a complex riddle, virtually staring at him from the wall of the physician's chamber. Cerdic's cryptic message, 'On an altar to your God and mine.' Pagan altars were supposed to be drenched in human gore; what had they to do with the crisp linen cloths where the Mass was celebrated? But Cerdic had not been talking about a marble slab or some blood-soaked plinth of stone. He had been taunting the Danes. They did have one thing in common: Christ had died on the wood of the cross while pagan priests often hung their sacrificial victims from the branches of oak trees.

Ralph controlled his excitement and stared out over the silent greenness. He could visualise Cerdic fleeing from the battle, coming here, to the makeshift stockade Brythnoth had set up. It was probably deserted, not a place to hide a precious treasure, so Cerdic had turned, fleeing to the spinney. Was the copse of trees the same in his day? Ralph frowned in thought. He had never noticed any forest clearance. As a boy he had climbed some of the great oaks; two or three of them had hollow trunks. Cerdic must have gone there. Oak trees survived for hundreds of years. Brythnoth's cross was in Devil's Spinney!

Ralph heard his name being called and looked down. Father Aylred was gazing up at him.

'Ralph,' he called. 'If I say a Mass in Midnight Tower would you be my altar boy?'

Ralph nodded and, nursing his secret, hurried down the steps.

'When will you say the Mass?'

Father Aylred looked calm, more composed. 'Soon,' he replied. 'What were you doing up on the parapet, Ralph?' He stepped closer. 'What's wrong? Your face is pale, your eyes are bright. Do you know who the killer is?'

'Not yet, Father, but God does!'

Chapter 5

'Why can't I intervene?' Beatrice stared desperately as her lover and Father Aylred walked back across the green. 'What are we?' she screamed at Brother Antony who watched her, his eyes full of compassion.

'Beatrice, you are an Incorporeal. I have told you. You are not of their world but of another.'

'But I can speak, I can see, I can hear, I have my body!'

'Yes, you have,' he said kindly. 'But they have all changed.'

'That's not possible.'

'Yes it is, Beatrice. Even in the world you have left, one substance can take many forms. Water can turn to ice, it can be still or fast-running; it can be small, it can be large, it can be salt-filled, it can be clear. It rises and it comes down. So it is with you. Your body has not been taken away, it has simply changed, as your consciousness has.'

Beatrice gazed around. The strange coppery tint had grown in strength. She was becoming accustomed to her new world.

143

She even knew how to rest, to withdraw into a warm darkness, shutting off her consciousness, asleep but not asleep. Nevertheless, she was growing frantic. This existence was like watching a mummer's play or studying the tale told on some tapestry. She had not seen the attack on Ralph in Devil's Spinney but she had become aware of his cries and, within the twinkling of an eye, she had been there. She had pulled down the briar so he could grasp it, she was sure she had! Or had it been a breeze or simply some subtle treachery of this strange light? She did not know who had attacked him, and she did not see the killer who had struck from the Salt Tower. She had seen Beardsmore fall and the wraiths gather to collect his soul. She had wanted to move, discover the identity of the mysterious assassin but she had been too terrified to leave Ralph. She had been with him in the green-filled darkness beneath the moat. And in the Salt Tower she had known of Eleanora's death, heard her heart-rending cries as her soul was taken off. Deep in her mind, Beatrice believed that knowledge of the killer was deliberately forbidden her. If she had kept her wits and tried to find out his identity, some obstacle would have arisen, as it had when Cerdic disappeared.

'Can't I intervene?' she asked.

Brother Antony smiled. 'In a way you can but that is something you must earn, Mistress Arrowner.' He touched her gently on the lips. The silver disc now shone at the back of his head, a circle of gleaming light. 'Be careful. Remember what I said about the Minstrel Man.' He walked away then disappeared as if into thin air.

Beatrice stood staring across the green. She was changing, becoming more powerful. She was fully aware of herself; she accepted that she was dead but her determination had grown. She was aware of her own will thrusting out, wishing to intervene, to protect the man she so dearly loved and had so tragically lost.

'Are you well, Beatrice Arrowner?'

Crispin and Clothilde were next to her, hands joined. They stood like beautiful twins smiling at her.

'Brother Antony warned me against you.'

'Of course he did.' Clothilde threw her head back and laughed, a tinkling sound. 'He is the guardian of the waste-lands. It is his task to keep you in order.' Clothilde pointed to the sentries on the parapet walk. 'Just like they protect the castle.'

'You promised to help me.'

'And in time we will,' Crispin replied languidly. 'But we must have your trust, Beatrice. Everything in life, and in death, has a price; it must be earned, must be bought. Nothing is free.'

'What is it you want?'

'Your trust, Beatrice. Here we are,' Crispin stretched out and stroked her hair, 'willing to help and yet you stand like a wench in the marketplace studying us as if we are hucksters!'

'What is happening in Midnight Tower?' Beatrice asked, trying to distract herself from Crispin's light-blue eyes.

'The priest summed up the truth of it. Spiritual life is, as

Brother Antony says, akin to water. In most people, and in most places, it lies sluggish like a lazy river at the height of summer, then something stirs its depths.' Crispin's face became excited. 'It grows stronger and fuller. The currents beneath pull and tug and the surface is disturbed.'

Beatrice studied these silver-haired twins. She wanted to believe what they said. They looked so beautiful. Brother Antony was so plain. All he could give was good advice while horrors bubbled around the man she loved and threatened to engulf him.

'Who is the killer?' she demanded.

'In time, Mistress Arrowner.'

She turned away in disgust and, before they could stop her, ran towards the wall, through it and out into the heathland. She reached Devil's Spinney and walked among the great oak trees. She had been with Ralph on the parapet walk. She had heard his whispers. She knew what he had discovered. This was an ancient place. She had become accustomed to the shapes and shadows, those strange priests with their ivy garlands and bronze, sickle knives, the terrible sacrifices they made to their demons. Even now they were clustered, chanting in a tongue she could not understand. Other phantasms appeared: that terrible knight in armour, his band of robbers around him, hanging some unfortunate peasant, drowning others in the marsh. They sat on their horses and laughed as the unfortunates shrieked for mercy before disappearing into the green, dark slime. Such phantasms no longer troubled her. Brother Antony had explained that they were mere shadows of what had been. Now and again she encountered the occasional wandering soul. Never a child but sometimes a man or woman lost in their own world, disturbed, distracted, unwilling to go on. She was also conscious of those beings who met the souls of the dead, the seraphim, glowing orbs of light, and the wraiths clustered together like monks chanting their psalter, and the demons, mailed men, knights in armour, hunting for souls.

'Mistress Arrowner!'

Two figures stepped out from the trees. Beatrice recognised Robin and Isabella, a young man and his wife. She had met them here before. They had explained how, many years ago, they had owned a tavern on the Maldon road, which had been burnt by French corsairs who brought their galleys up the Blackwater estuary before riding inland. They were merry souls, unable really to explain why they had not moved on.

'Perhaps we loved this world,' Isabella had laughed. 'We had such a good life, Beatrice. Robin served ales and wines while I cooked in the kitchens. On one occasion we even served the King.' She blinked. 'I forget his name . . .'

Beatrice had come to accept them. They always appeared hand in hand, chattering incessantly about the petty things of their lives, what they had done, whom they had met.

'What are you doing here?' Robin came forward, thumb stuck in the belt round his green jerkin, his brown leggings pushed into strange-looking boots. He was clean-shaven and had smiling brown eyes beneath his auburn hair. Isabella looked similar but thinner, more prone to laughter than her husband.

Beatrice told them everything she had learnt.

'Then why don't we help?' Isabella suggested.

'Is that possible?' Beatrice asked.

'If Brythnoth's cross is here,' said Robin, 'at least we can look at it. There's nothing wrong with that.'

Beatrice was distracted by shadows flitting across the skies like dark clouds. 'I should go back to the castle,' she murmured. 'I really shouldn't leave Ralph. He's in danger, you know . . .'

'Stay for a while,' Isabella soothed. 'Stay here, Beatrice. Let's search for Brythnoth's cross.'

'But where can we begin?' Beatrice asked. The shadows were lengthening and, because she wanted to, she felt the growing coldness of the air. 'Have you met Crispin and Clothilde?'

'Oh yes, on many occasions,' Robin smiled. 'A precious pair, them!'

'They said that one day I could learn how to intervene in the world of the living, make my presence felt.'

'Oh, we can do that.'

Beatrice started in surprise.

'We can,' Isabella confirmed, grasping her hand. 'Come, Beatrice, we'll show you.'

'What about Brythnoth's cross?'

'Oh, leave that,' Robin laughed. 'If, as you say, it is in Devil's Spinney then it will stay there for a little while longer.'

'But what about Ralph?' Beatrice looked longingly towards the barbican.

'Don't you want to intervene?' Isabella asked.

'Come away, Mistress!' Brother Antony was suddenly standing on the trackway glaring angrily at her. 'Come away, Beatrice!' He lifted a hand, dark and threatening against the blue sky.

'Oh, just ignore him!' Isabella hissed mischievously. 'Where would you like to go, Beatrice?'

Beatrice experienced a cold blast of air. Brother Antony appeared to have grown larger. He stood with his hands hanging by his sides, staring fixedly at her. Beatrice suddenly resented his lecturing, his vague promises, his constant watching of her.

'The Pot of Thyme!' she declared defiantly, shouting the words as if she wanted Brother Antony to hear. 'Let's go to the Pot of Thyme!'

She ran, Robin and Isabella clasping her hands. They hastened across the heathland like children playing some game. Robin and Isabella were laughing, squeezing Beatrice's hands. They passed the churchyard and Beatrice paused. Usually God's acre stretched out, a mixture of headstones and weather-beaten crosses among high-growing grass and old yew trees, gnarled and bent, their branches stretching out. A quiet, serene place. Beatrice stared in horror. It had all gone. Instead she was looking down an icy-white valley, high banks of snow on either side with a pathway stretching to the light-blue horizon. At the end of the valley a fiery sun glowed as it dipped into the west. On either side of the valley an army of shadows thronged. What really caught Beatrice's attention was the figure coming along the pathway. Two great hounds bounded before him, barking loudly, their great ears flapping as they dived in and out of the snow. The figure drew nearer. He looked like a chapman with his sumpter pony. He was dressed in vari-coloured garments on which little bells jingled at every step. Beatrice glanced quickly at her companions. Robin and Isabella were kneeling, foreheads against the ground.

'What is it?' she gasped, feeling a fear she had never experienced since that dreadful fall from the parapet walk. 'Robin, Isabella, what is it?'

She was aware of singing, the deep-throated voices of the shadows on either side of the valley chanting a paean of praise. Robin and Isabella still knelt, heads down. Beatrice again looked at the valley but it had gone, the snow, the trackway, the mysterious jingling figure and those fierce barking hounds.

'What happened?' Beatrice demanded. 'I saw snow, a pedlar!'

Isabella was now on her feet, face glowing, eyes sparkling. 'Oh, it's only a friend of ours.'

Beatrice felt uneasy. 'But why did you kneel?' She looked again at the graveyard where grey shapes moved among the tombstones like tendrils of mist on a spring morning.

'You'll see,' said Robin. 'But forget the dead, Beatrice, the living await.'

Beatrice remained fixed to the spot. The graveyard was now full of those silver discs, shining and shimmering. They formed a path as a golden sphere left the church, rising up in the air and then back down again. Beatrice was sure the golden sphere, or whatever was in it, was staring directly at her. She had learnt how to experience, to feel, to stretch out her mind. She closed her eyes and experienced a deep warmth, a loving embrace, as when she and Ralph used to lie together in the grass and stare up at the sky. Then the sphere disappeared and Brother Antony was standing on a tombstone like some huge, forbidding black raven, gesturing at her to come closer.

'No, come with us, Beatrice,' Robin whispered. 'And you'll learn something. You'll find the power that he denies you.'

Beatrice was about to refuse, then she recalled her helplessness as Ralph struggled in the mire and, turning away, she joined the other two in their wild flight along the cobbled high street of Maldon.

The Pot of Thyme's taproom was filling with customers. Beatrice was acutely aware something was wrong. She had visited the tavern on a number of occasions. It was usually friendly, the meeting place of travelling people, chapmen, tinkers, pedlars, wandering scholars, itinerant friars. None of these was present now. Only peasants, villeins, cottagers, young men from the village and the surrounding hamlets. Taylis coldly turned away anyone else. The men were gathered round the overturned casks which served as tables. Beatrice noticed that the trap door to the cellars beneath had been opened; one of the pot boys was bringing out quivers of arrows, bows, helmets, pikes and hauberks. Martin the miller was there, his face wet with in tears. Others tried to comfort him.

'Come on,' Isabella urged. 'Let's see what mischief we can cause.'

'No, no, let me stay here. What's happening?' Beatrice sensed the resentment, hatred and grudges curdling in these men's hearts.

'It's only a cauldron,' Robin whispered. 'Coming to bubble – it will spill over soon enough.'

Beatrice would not be moved. She stood in the corner. The ugly mood of the gathering was apparent and audible in the muttered curses about the King's taxmen, the castle, and Sir John Grasse. After Taylis closed and barred the door, he went and stood in the middle of the room, banging his staff against the wooden floorboards.

'When Adam delved and Eve span, who was then the gentleman?'

The doggerel lines were taken up in a roar.

'Worms of the earth, that's what the great lords of the dunghill call us!' shouted Taylis. 'We are tied to the soil, we are heavily taxed and now our young men and women are killed. Fulk in the moat, Eleanora in some filthy dungeon.'

'Eye for eye, tooth for tooth, life for life!' an old man chanted, saliva dripping from his gumless mouth.

'There's trouble at the castle,' someone else observed. 'Fulk and Eleanora are not the only ones to die.'

The words created a moment of silence.

'What are you saying, Piers?' Martin the miller demanded.

Beatrice smiled as Piers clambered to his feet. He was a good, strong man, clear-eyed and honest-faced. When she was a child, Piers used to dandle her on his knee and tell her tales about wicked goblins and elves.

'I think we should take good counsel,' Piers declared vehemently. 'Master Taylis is right, the lords of the dunghill oppress us so I do not speak for them. The royal tax collectors are nothing but jackdaws which hunt for anything that glitters. I do not speak for them either.' His blunt eloquence brought murmurs of approval.

'But I do think we should be careful and take prudent counsel.'

'You haven't lost a son,' Martin the miller jibed.

'No, but I loved Beatrice Arrowner. She was a comely, kindly lass. Master Ralph the castle clerk loved her as well. What I am saying is this: Goodman Winthrop's murder was a mistake. The soldiers will come from London and they'll not rest until they see two or three of us hang. Have you ever seen men throttled at the crossroads? Do you want to see your sons' corpses picked and clawed at by the birds of the air?' He paused, his cold words of warning dousing the anger in their hearts.

'We will put our trust in our brethren from Essex and Kent!' a farmer shouted.

'Oh, aye,' Piers taunted. 'And when de Spencer, Bishop of Norwich, comes marching south with his mercenaries, burning our houses, pillaging our goods, raping our wives and daughters, will they come to our help then? This will end in blood and tears.' He pointed a finger at Taylis. 'You're planning an attack on the castle, aren't you?'

'At night,' the taverner replied, 'we'll take the place by force, burn it to the ground.'

Piers walked closer. 'And what will you do with Sir John and Lady Anne? Hang them in Devil's Spinney? What about Master Ralph? Adam? The soldiers and men-at-arms? They are lads like us. And do you think they'll give up their lives lightly?' Piers spread his hands. 'Brothers, what wrong has Sir John Grasse done to us? He's a kindly man.'

Beatrice felt relieved at the nods of agreement. Piers was much respected. He had served in the Black Prince's retinue in France. He knew what he was talking about. Beatrice joined her hands in prayer. If these men attacked the castle, they would show no mercy, leave no witnesses. If only she could warn Ralph. She felt so hopeless and frightened. She stared around. That strange bronze light also glowed in the taproom; she was aware of dark shadows, like plumes of smoke, rising, moving in and out among the men. She glanced at her companions.

'What is this?'

She did not like the expression on their faces, eyes glittering, lips parted as if they were enjoying the spectacle, like people watching a bear being baited.

'They spit out the slime of Hell,' Robin declared.

Beatrice looked again but the taproom had disappeared.

She stood on the edge of a great forest. She was aware of the trees around her as she stared across a plain whose burning sand could nourish no roots. It was ringed by red hills. Herds of naked men and women were being driven across it, eyes burning with their scalding tears. Some had fallen to the ground, others squatted with their arms about them. The air dinned with their hideous lamentations. Men-at-arms, wielding whips, whirled round this herd like hunters would frightened deer. The sky turned an orange colour then the image disappeared. It was replaced by that freezing snow-filled valley. The pedlar with his jingling bells was drawing nearer. The pack pony was like some giant hare with elongated ears and fiery eyes. The mastiffs loped ahead, their barking like the clanging of some deep bell. On the rim of the valley, the army was more distinct: legion after legion of garishly-garbed soldiers, their cry ringing up: 'Power and glory! All praise!' The vision disappeared. She was back in the tavern: Piers was holding forth and winning his comrades over. The taproom had become divided, the majority, particularly the older ones, accepting Piers's words of caution. Taylis the taverner's face was mottled with fury as he tried to regain the ground he had lost. A vote was taken: the castle would not be attacked. Martin the miller sprang to his feet.

'And what about my son?'

'Leave that to the royal justices,' Piers snapped. 'Better still, I'll approach Sir John.'

And on such words the meeting broke up. Some of the

younger men gathered round the taverner; their muttered curses and surly looks showed they had not accepted what had been decided.

'Come with us, Beatrice.'

Her hands were grasped. Robin and Isabella sped with her across the taproom and up the stairs to a chamber. The room was dark and dingy. An unemptied chamber pot stood in the corner covered by a filthy cloth. A rickety table, two narrow stools and a broken coffer were the only items of furniture in the room. A man was sitting on the bed. A tavern wench, a slattern, was kneeling on the floor before him; it was obvious that the greasy-faced, pockmarked young man was attempting a clumsy seduction. He was dressed in a scruffy brown jerkin with dark-blue sleeves unbuttoned to reveal a wine-stained shirt beneath. His fat legs were encased in blue kersey leggings. On the floor beside him were his scuffed boots and a rather battered war belt from which sword and dagger hung. Against the bolsters were two bulging leather panniers full of yellowing scrolls of parchment. The wench was pretty enough, narrow-faced, with long, black hair which reached to her shoulders. The bodice of her bottle-green dress had been undone, revealing swelling breasts beneath a white chemise.

'Are you really what you say?' the wench asked, smiling at the silver coin the man twirled between his fingers.

'I have more power than you think,' the fellow replied. 'I am a summoner from the Archdeacon's Court of Arches. I have powers both natural and supernatural.'

'What does that mean?'

'I could have you summoned to the Archdeacon's Court for whoring and lechery.'

'Don't be impudent!' the wench snapped. 'Master Taylis sent me up because you wanted some company.'

The summoner scratched at a red spot on his cheek, taking away the pus-filled scab. 'How would you like to travel to Colchester and appear before the Archdeacon, eh? He is a terrible man. So,' he patted the bed beside him, 'why not sit here and entertain me?'

The wench obeyed. The summoner knocked his saddlebags full of writs and proclamations on to the floor and grasped the girl, rolling her on to the bed. He plunged a hand up her skirts, pulling back both kirtle and petticoat beneath. The girl kicked out long, brown legs, oohing and aahing as she thrust away his probing hands. Robin and Isabella were laughing but Beatrice did not like being here. It wasn't so much spying on these two as the atmosphere in the chamber. Those shapes she had seen in the taproom below moved about, the air was tinged with a rank smell like the stench from an unclean latrine. Beatrice could see the wench was repelled by the scabby-faced summoner but attracted by his silver. She sat up on the bed, her dress awry, her hair almost covering her face.

'Give me the silver piece,' she demanded.

The summoner tossed it on to the table and grasped her by the arm.

'It will stay there until I have had my pleasure.' He paused at the sound of voices from the taproom below. 'What's happening below?' he asked.

'Oh, the usual grumbles.'

'I heard rumours about a tax collector being murdered.'

'Yes,' the wench replied, enjoying the look of fear on the summoner's face. 'He came here collecting what he shouldn't.'

'Not like me,' the summoner replied. 'I pay for what I take.'

'What about these powers?' the wench asked. 'What do you mean by supernatural?'

'I have powers,' the summoner replied, holding one hand up, fingers splayed.

Robin and Isabella were now giggling like two mischievous children.

'I can call on the Dark Lords to do my bidding.'

'And do what?' the wench asked.

'Things. I can make matter move without touching it.'

Isabella darted forward and knocked a tin cup off the table; Robin picked up the war belt and flung it across the room. The summoner stared, mouth open, eyes popping.

'You can do it!' said the wench, awed.

'I . . . er . . .' The summoner was alarmed.

Robin and Isabella were enjoying their game. They pulled a cloak off a peg and tossed it to the floor. They picked up the grimy towel from the lavarium and waved it like a pennant. The wench was now frightened. She climbed off the bed and retreated to the door. Isabella was ready for her, pulling across the bolts and turning the key. Other items were picked up and thrown like scraps of straw.

The summoner paled with fright, beads of sweat ran down his cheek. He was so taken by the terrors that he wet himself. He sat rigid, hands on his knees. The maid began to scream.

'Stop it!' Beatrice called. 'For the love of God, stop it!'

Immediately Robin and Isabella became docile and stood with their hands at their sides, heads lowered, looking at her from under their brows. Their eyes seemed to have lost their colour. The tavern wench drew back the bolts, flung open the door and went screaming down the gallery. The summoner moved quickly, grasping at his possessions, putting the silver coin back in his purse. He threw himself through the open doorway. Robin and Isabella laughed.

'You see, Beatrice,' Isabella crowed, grasping her husband's hand. 'Brother Antony was wrong. You can cross the divide. You could intervene.'

'How?' she asked.

'Let your hate flow,' Robin replied with a smile. 'Think of it as a stick or a dagger, put all your mind, heart and soul behind it.'

Beatrice stared at this precious pair. What they offered was tantalising but she sensed there was something dreadfully wrong about it, that if she accepted what they said, there would be no turning back.

'I want to go,' she said.

'Beatrice! Beatrice Arrowner!'

She looked through the window. Brother Antony stood in the street below, shaking a raised finger in warning.

Beatrice fled from the room, down the steps. But outside there was no high street, no Brother Antony, only a long, dark trackway fringed by trees. The chapman leading his sumpter pony, the two great mastiffs bounding before him, was coming towards her.

Words Between the Pilgrims

The clerk paused in his tale. The pilgrims clustered round the crackling fire beseeched him with their eyes to continue. The pardoner, clawing at his flaxen hair, was smirking mischievously at the summoner who sat, head down, shoulders hunched.

'Have you ever been to Maldon, sir?' The pardoner asked sweetly.

'Never!' this messenger of the Church snapped. 'I've never been to Maldon. I know nothing of a tavern called the Pot of Thyme.' Yet the way he moved his lips and a shift in his eyes showed the pilgrims he was lying. The man of law hitched his fur robes tighter round his shoulders. This tale disturbed him, and so did this God-forsaken wood, with the mist seeping in, the sounds of the night all around them. Only the fiery warmth of the fire kept the terrors at bay.

'I've been to Maldon,' the reeve announced, looking quickly at the knight. Sir Godfrey hid a smile behind his hand. He knew all about the reeve's activities in the great revolt that had swept through Essex and Kent some nine years previously: the reeve had been high in the rebels' council.

'I recognise some of the names,' the reeve continued in his nasal whine. 'The farmer, Piers, Taylis the taverner, though he's now dead.'

'These visions you describe, Master Clerk,' Sir Godfrey said, 'can you explain them?'

Surprisingly, the monk leaned forward, one bony hand extended as a sign that he wished to speak.

'There are many worlds,' he said in a deep, rich voice. 'How do we know that five or six realities don't exist at the same time? Even the great philosophers admit to such a possibility.'

'And do you think,' the knight asked, 'that there are creatures who can pass through the twilight?'

'Why, of course, Sir Godfrey,' the monk replied softly. 'And they come for many reasons.' He bared his teeth.

The wife of Bath flinched at the sight of his sharp dog's teeth.

'In death as in life, there are hunters and hunted.'

'Aye,' Sir Godfrey replied. 'And it is as well to know which is which.'

The monk glanced away.

'I would like to know,' the wife of Bath chirped up, 'if this is a true story, or at least which strands of it are true. How do you know what Beatrice saw?' She studied the clerk's soft face. In the flickering firelight he looked very handsome and the wife of Bath wetted her lips. It had been so long since she had bounced merrily on a bed. The clerk did not answer her question. He looked round at his audience and said, 'Prepare your minds, kind sirs and ladies, for the Lords of Hell!'

PART III

Chapter 1

Beatrice stood and watched the man on his sumpter pony draw nearer and, as he did so, the snow-filled valley and the hounds disappeared. Once again he looked like an ordinary chapman on the high road of Maldon, his pony a bedraggled mount with bulging panniers and baskets on either side. The man was tall, now soberly dressed in a brown leather jerkin and brown leggings. His blue cloak was gathered behind him, fastened at the neck by a silver chain. A war belt round his slim waist carried sword and dagger. One hand held the reins, the other a stout walking staff. He had a handsome face, deep-set eyes, sharp nose and a merry mouth. His black moustache and beard were neatly clipped. Beatrice noticed that his fingers were long, the nails carefully cut. On one wrist he wore a gold band, on the other a leather guard. He stopped in front of her.

'Beatrice Arrowner?' He smiled, showing teeth that were white and even. The little bells sewn to his jerkin tinkled musically at his every movement.

'Who are you?' Beatrice asked. 'I can see you and you can see me. Are you a ghost?'

'I'm the Minstrel Man.'

'And where are you going, sir?' Beatrice was too curious to heed Brother Antony's warning.

'Why, Beatrice, the same as you, Ravenscroft Castle.'

'But are you a ghost?' she insisted.

He slipped the staff through a cord in the saddle of his sumpter pony and grasped her hand.

'Come with me, Beatrice. I've been invited there. I've heard the summons. I want to see what songs can be sung, stories told, webs woven.' He squeezed her hand; his touch was very warm. Beatrice felt calm and peaceful; and it seemed only natural to walk with him. Soon she was chattering like a child, telling him everything that had happened. The Minstrel Man was a good listener. When she fell silent, he began to sing a song softly under his breath, a heart-catching tune though Beatrice did not understand the guttural words.

'What words are they?' she asked.

'Ah, it's an ancient song.' The Minstrel Man paused and turned to face her. 'I've sung it many a time, before the soaring monuments of Egypt, the hanging gardens of Babylon, the great towers of Troy and the golden palaces of the Byzantine.'

'You've travelled far?' she asked.

'I travel, Mistress, wherever I'm invited.' His reply was soft, followed by a slow wink of the eye.

'And what will you do at Ravenscroft?'

'Why, Beatrice, make music.'

'But they won't hear you!'

'Oh, they will. The song I sing has been heard many times.'

Beatrice felt a tinge of apprehension. She noticed how dark the highway had become and something else: in the fields on either side the grazing cattle were moving away and all birdsong had ceased. There was no crackling or bustling in the thicket. She stared back in the direction of Maldon. Shadows clustered there as if an army of the dead were following them. Nothing substantial, just those black plumes of smoke she had glimpsed from the taproom of the Pot of Thyme, now gathering together. Above her the sky was streaked with dark-red clouds.

'So, what do you want?' the Minstrel Man asked.

'To help Ralph. Robin and Isabella said I could have that power.'

'Of course you can.' The Minstrel Man's voice was a purr. 'Do you remember Ralph in the mire struggling to get out? If you had wanted to, if you had really tried, you could have grasped his hand and plucked him out.'

'Could I?'

The Minstrel Man looked down the trackway and whistled under his breath. 'Come, Beatrice, I'll show you.'

They rounded a corner. To the side of the trackway stood a small cart. The horse had been unhitched and the Moon people – a man, two women and a child dressed in motley rags – had gathered bracken and lit a fire against the approaching night.

One of the women was skinning a rabbit and cleaning out the entrails before packing the meat with herbs and putting it on a makeshift spit over the fire. The Minstrel Man left his horse and walked towards them, still grasping Beatrice's hand. Immediately, the older woman, with yellowing skin and greying hair, looked up, eyes rounded. She spoke in a strange tongue to the man, whose hand went clumsily for the dagger in his belt. Their horse, a docile-looking cob, hobbled some yards away, reared and whinnied. The young boy ran to his mother. She clasped him, wrapping her arms round him. All were staring fixedly, their terror tangible.

'Can they see us?' Beatrice asked.

'No,' the Minstrel Man replied. 'But they know I'm here.'

The old woman held up her hand, thumb pushed between her fingers as she made the sign to ward off evil.

'Just ignore their little game,' the Minstrel Man murmured.

The touch of his hand had gone cold. Beatrice's unease deepened. The Moon man crouched down and placed his dagger on a piece of wood. He, too, had one hand extended, moving it slowly backwards and forwards as if trying to reassure whatever was around him.

'Look at that dagger,' the Minstrel Man murmured. 'Go on, Beatrice, look at it!'

She obeyed.

'Think of Ralph. Think of that killer waiting in the shadow on the parapet walk.' He was now behind her, one hand on her shoulder. 'It wasn't fair, was it, Beatrice?' His voice had taken on a sing-song tone. 'It wasn't fair to be thrust out of life, to be sent flying into the night air, smashing into the ground below. And why should it happen to you? You were a good girl, Beatrice. Good to your aunt and your uncle. Good to the church. You deserved long life. It was your right to lie naked in Ralph's arms. To be his handfast, to bear his children.'

Beatrice felt a deep sadness.

'Look across the field, Beatrice.'

She did so. Instead of green grass she saw a smartly-painted house and a cobbled yard. She and Ralph were sitting on a bench against the wall. A small boy, dressed in a little green shift, was staggering around, his fat face creased in a smile. He held a wooden sword in his chubby hands. He was chuckling with glee. Ralph was teasing him, telling him to come closer. When the young boy did, Ralph pretended to be a dragon. The little lad laughed and ran away. Beatrice watched herself get up, put the piece of embroidery down and run after the child. She picked him up, clasping him to her. Beatrice moaned at the sweetness of it all.

'This is your life,' the Minstrel Man said. 'This was cruelly taken from you. A long and happy life in which you gave love and love was returned. How could God do that? Why should an assassin get away with it? Hurry now. Ralph is waiting.'

'What do I do? What do I do?'

'Take the knife.' He pushed Beatrice gently across the grass.

'I can't touch it.'

'Think, Beatrice,' He said 'Think of vengeance. Think of

justice. Think of Ralph. Take the knife, pick it up, show thes
fools that they are in the presence of someone great.'

Beatrice went forward. She grasped the knife but she coul
feel nothing.

'Think of the assassin,' the Minstrel Man urged. 'Think o
the murderer laughing and joking, of the long years ahead
of Ralph lying in the arms of another. Of that child you'
never see.'

Beatrice felt a spurt of anger go through her like dy
colouring water. She lunged and plucked the knife up. Sh
looked round; the Minstrel Man was smiling.

'There you go, Beatrice. There's my bonny lass.'

The Moon people were staring transfixed. The youn
woman began to shriek, clutching the boy close to her.

'Silence her!' The voice seemed to come from within her
'Silence her, Beatrice! Let loose the power you have withi
you. You have so much power, Beatrice, that's why I hav
travelled to meet you.'

She took a step forward. The man was crouched on th
ground, arms wrapped round himself, whimpering like
dog. The old crone squatted as if she had been turne
to stone. The young woman rent the air with her terribl
screams.

'Shut her up!' The words came in a snarl.

Abruptly one of those silver discs of light came betwee
Beatrice and the woman and then moved away. The youn
boy broke free. He approached the knife, his eyes large an
dark above tear-soaked cheeks.

'Please!' He mouthed the words. 'Please don't hurt us! We didn't mean to steal the rabbit!'

Beatrice's resolve crumbled. She put the knife gently on the ground and stretched out her hand to touch the child's cheek. For a moment she felt wet skin, a wisp of hair.

'Don't you worry,' she soothed. 'Don't you worry, little one.'

'Beatrice Arrowner!'

She glanced round. The Minstrel Man was standing, legs apart, an ugly snarl on his face.

'You stupid wench! You foolish bitch! You whine, you beg and, when you have the power, you throw it away as if it was a dirty rag!'

He took a step forward. A silver disc came between him and Beatrice. The Minstrel Man smirked. He spoke in that strange guttural tongue. The disc moved away. The Minstrel Man snatched the reins of his pony and the animal raised its head. Beatrice recoiled in horror; it was no longer a sumpter pony but a shape with black hair, long ears, snarling mouth, fiery eyes.

'Farewell, Beatrice Arrowner.' The Minstrel Man waggled a finger at her. 'I still have company to keep at Ravenscroft.' And, whistling under his breath, he and his ghoulish mount walked away along the track. He lifted a hand in farewell but didn't turn his head.

'Beatrice Arrowner! I told you to be careful!' Brother Antony was standing under a tree. He came towards her and grasped her by the hand. 'Stay well away from him.'

'I thought he could help.'

'You thought he could help!' Brother Antony shook his head sadly. 'Do you realise what he was urging you to do, Beatrice?'

'I wanted to help,' she stammered.

He took her away across the track. Behind them the Moon people were more composed, talking among themselves, intent on moving camp as quickly as possible. Brother Antony and Beatrice watched them go then he leaned over and kissed her on the cheek.

'Why did you do that?' Beatrice asked, surprised.

'You've been tested and you have not been found wanting.' Brother Antony smiled. 'I told you, Beatrice, where you are now is just the same as life.' He tapped her on the head and on the heart. 'The intellect and the will are all that matter. Now the games are over. Robin and Isabella? They are demons.'

'No!' Yet she could tell from the grave expression on his face that he was telling the truth.

'They are demons,' Antony repeated. 'They are the same as Crispin and Clothilde. In fact, they are one and the same being, manifesting themselves in either sex, assuming many forms. They were sent to tempt you. To entice you into the darkness. To hate, to seek vengeance. To argue constantly with God like their master does.'

'And the Minstrel Man?' Beatrice asked.

'One of the great Lords of Hell, Dominus Achitophel. A great baron of the fiery pit, one of Satan's tenants-in-chief

He wanders the wastelands which are both freezing and hot while the hordes of Hell pay him tribute.'

Beatrice repressed her fear. 'But why would such a baron have anything to do with me?'

'For two reasons. Yours is a soul still out for capture and a soul full of power. Satan, in the very depths of his hate, is always attracted by such souls.'

'But the Minstrel Man said he was still going to Ravenscroft.'

Brother Antony smiled sadly. 'Beatrice, most sins are the result of human weakness, of weariness and frustration. A man becomes tired of ploughing the soil, of watching his bairns starve, of his wife shrivel before his eyes. So he drinks too much. He doesn't control his lusts. But that's not badness, wickedness, just human frailty. Or take those who rob. Many are brought up in abject poverty, they know no different.' Brother Antony's face seemed to become smoother and younger, a faraway look in his eyes. 'The compassion of Christ is all-understanding. In the end, Beatrice, God's love will invade this world. It will sweep away, it will turn back, it will heal. At the end of time, when the heavens crack with fire, time will run back and God will make all things well.' He paused and said something softly in Latin, staring up at the sky. 'God is coming again, Beatrice. He has counted and weighed the tear of every child, the loneliest cry of pain. He has noted every injustice under the sun, and there will be a reckoning.' His voice rose, his eyes bright. 'Every time a child is abused, God is abused. Every time a woman is raped, God is raped. Every time an injustice

171

is committed, God is violated. All these things must b
put right.'

'So why does the Minstrel Man go to Ravenscroft?'

'The Minstrel Man sings a demonic hymn.' Brother Antony
stepped closer. 'He's attracted by the real evil there, tru
wickedness, a human soul, a being comfortable, endowed wit
talents, deliberately and maliciously plotting then carrying ou
dreadful murders. For what?'

'I don't know. Brythnoth's cross?'

'Perhaps. But, it's not just greed. Other darker sins run i
harness with it: an enjoyment, a malicious desire. A nightmar
soul has sung its song and Hell has answered.'

'Do you know who the assassin is?' Beatrice asked.

Brother Antony shook his head. 'The all-seeing God knows
But God depends on us, Beatrice. On those who have th
means, and the will, to see justice done.'

'But the Minstrel Man threatened Ralph.'

Brother Antony shook his head. 'Ralph's soul and life li
in the hand of God.'

'Like mine did,' Beatrice declared. Her voice shook wit
emotion. 'I saw that vision of my future.'

'But was it the truth?' Brother Antony retorted. 'I tel
you this, Beatrice, what God has prepared for you an
Ralph, when his justice is done, will compensate for th
evil and wickedness you have suffered. Trust in him, trus
in me.' He grasped her hands. 'Promise me, Beatrice, no
you have been tested, now you have chosen for yoursel
that never again will you listen to Crispin and Clothilde

Robin and Isabella. Or whatever other demon Hell spits out.'

'I promise.' Beatrice turned away.

'Where are you going, Mistress?'

'Why, Brother, to Ravenscroft.'

He pointed down the road at the retreating party of Moon people.

'But you have done an injustice, reparation is demanded.'

'If I could, Brother Antony, I would do anything. That poor child, the terror in his eyes . . .'

Brother Antony seized her by the hand. 'Come on, let's catch up.'

They seemed to cover the separating distance in a twinkling of an eye. Brother Antony pulled Beatrice on to the tail of the cart. Beatrice could sense the Moon people's fear.

'What do I do?' she asked.

'Think!' Brother Antony hissed. 'Forget yourself. Try and put yourself in the place of each of them.'

'What do they do?'

'The man is a tinker. I can only help you so much. You must do it for yourself. You cannot enter their souls but pain is self-evident. Put yourself in their place. Think of the other, Beatrice Arrowner, forget yourself. Let your mind slip.'

Beatrice did so.

'Stare at each of them.'

Beatrice obeyed. She first looked at the young woman holding the boy. She saw how tired her face was, heavy-eyed, the constant gnawing of the lip. She felt herself slip into what the woman was fearful of. The Moon woman had forgotten the terrifying experience, she was more concerned with something practical.

'She's frightened for the man,' Beatrice declared. 'She's worried about him.'

'What is she worried about?'

Once again Beatrice immersed herself, and this time it was easier. She discovered the Moon woman was the man's wife, the older woman her mother. She experienced their courage in the face of hardship, their deep devotion to each other and their unspoken fears.

'He's a good tinker,' she said, 'an honest man who looks after her and her aged mother.'

'And what are they worried about, Beatrice Arrowner?'

'Two months ago he injured his right wrist and it hasn't healed properly. He cannot hold the hammer and they fear for the future.'

Beatrice moved through the cart and sat next to the man on the rough driver's seat. His face was sweat-soaked, his right hand dangling in his lap. He was having difficulty holding the reins. Now and again, eyes half-closed, he would wince with pain.

'His wrist is really hurting him,' Beatrice said. 'And he wants to hide this from the others.'

'Think of his wrist, Beatrice.'

Beatrice did. She felt a fiery pain shoot through her own arm and her fingers went limp.

'Oh, what can I do?' she cried. 'I'd do anything!'

'Hold his wrist!'

Beatrice did so. She felt a deep compassion for this poor tinker. She forgot about herself, about Ralph, Ravenscroft, the Minstrel Man. All she was aware of was the fear and pain mingling in the tinker's mind. She kept rubbing his wrist, pushing with her fingers, willing it to be better. Brother Antony was talking but she ignored him. She felt dreadfully sad that she had frightened such a man and deeply concerned that she had stirred up his anxieties.

'I am sorry,' she whispered into his ear. 'I am so very, very sorry.'

She felt a fire within her. If she could only break out. She had now grasped the man's wrist between both hands. The horse seemed to sense something and picked up speed. The man became alarmed. Beatrice was aware of a silver disc passing between her and the tinker. The horse shied. The cart hit a rut and lurched. The man screamed as his damaged wrist caught the wooden seat.

'Oh no!' Beatrice cried.

But then the tinker was pulling at the reins to halt the horse. He raised his right arm, flexing his fingers. Beatrice felt a deep exhaustion as if she had been drained of all energy. She panicked at what might be happening. The tinker, meanwhile, was staring in stupefaction. Once again Beatrice tried to sense what he was feeling. She experienced a deep sense of relief, an absence of pain. The tinker, to the amazement of his family, jumped down from the cart and started waving his arms. He was jabbering in a tongue she couldn't understand. The two women were laughing and crying at the same time.

'It's healed, isn't it?' Beatrice said. 'It's a miracle.'

'Of sorts,' Brother Antony replied. 'But what's a miracle, Beatrice? His wrist was dislocated. The cart jolted, his wrist received a blow and the joint was realigned.'

'I feel so tired,' she said wearily. 'Why should I feel tired? I have no body.'

'Yes, you have,' Brother Antony replied. 'But it's incorporeal. You have given him your strength, the power of your will.'

He sat down beneath a tree and indicated that she should do likewise. They watched the tinker embrace his wife and the old woman, and hug the child.

'Our prayers are answered,' the tinker declared in a tongue she could understand. 'So now to Ravenscroft where Sir John always has good trade for me.'

They all climbed back on the cart. Beatrice watched them go. Brother Antony put an arm round her; unresistingly she allowed him to put her head on his shoulder.

'Surely I can't sleep,' she murmured.

'Rest,' he soothed. 'Think of the darkness, of warmth.'

Beatrice felt herself falling, then she shook herself. Brother Antony was gone. She was still seated under the tree, the daylight was fading. Hours must have passed but it felt like moments. She sprang to her feet. She thought of Ralph and hastened along the track . . .

She reached the crossroads. Etheldreda was squatting there

176

She glanced fearfully up at Beatrice. 'A great lord has passed,' she said.

'Leave her, Beatrice Arrowner.' Crispin and Clothilde had appeared on the other side of the crossroads. They were smiling at her. Beatrice recalled the Moon people, that terrible dagger scything the air, the abject tears of the little boy. She had had enough of this precious pair with their lies and deceit.

'Go away!' she screamed.

They stared back, eyebrows raised.

'In Christ's name,' Beatrice crossed herself, 'leave me alone!'

The two merged into one, then separated again, as Robin and Isabella. Their faces changed and, Beatrice glimpsed the mocking features of the Minstrel Man, before once again they became Crispin and Clothilde. Behind her Etheldreda was gibbering with fright.

'Hell's spawn!' Beatrice screamed. 'You lied to me! You tricked me!'

They turned away. Clothilde looked over her shoulder, her face no longer beautiful, eyes red like glowing coals, mouth twisted in a leer. She parted her lips and gave a hiss, a blast of fire. The searing gust of heat made Beatrice flinch and stagger back, then they were gone.

Beatrice waited for a while and, when her strength returned, made her way along the track. Ravenscroft's turrets and towers came into sight. She hastened across the drawbridge. She was aware of the Moon people's cart, the tinker's hammer clattering against the pots, the ordinary sights and sounds of a castle. The bailey, however, was also full of ghosts, two worlds co-existing. In the centre was the Minstrel Man and around him were grouped Black Malkyn, Lady Johanna, Crispin and Clothilde, kneeling in obeisance to this great Lord of Hell.

Chapter 2

Ralph entered his chamber and leaned against the door. He sniffed and, once again, caught the faint fragrance of Beatrice's perfume. He felt uneasy. The chamber was gloomy, the night candle flickering under its metal cap. He wondered if Beatrice was still with him.

'Are you there?' he called out but the only answer was the shutter rattling in the breeze. Ralph moved across to his writing desk and stared down at the manuscripts. He had deliberately said and written nothing about his discovery. Nevertheless, he was sure someone had been in here, sifting through the manuscripts, searching for something.

He opened the shutters and stared out. Later that evening Father Aylred was to celebrate Mass in the entrance to Midnight Tower. Everyone else was busy trying to do their work despite the oppressive atmosphere at Ravenscroft. Now was the best time to go. Ralph took his war belt from a peg and strapped it round his waist. He put on his cloak and left his chamber, locking the door behind him.

The castle bailey was deserted apart from the travelling Moon people. The man, a professional tinker by trade, seemed happy to be here, grateful to Sir John for bringing out the pots, pans and skillets that required attention.

Ralph quickly made his way across the green and into the Salt Tower. Sir John had still not followed his advice to protect this vulnerable part of the castle defences. He went up the steps, trying not to indulge in fanciful notions, yet it was hard. The assassin must have crept up here bringing those arbalests which had killed Beardsmore.

Ralph reached the first landing and walked into the chamber. The assassin had used that large window to smuggle poor Phoebe's corpse out of the castle. Now, Ralph intended to use it for his own secret purposes. He opened the large shutters and climbed carefully out. The day had been a dull one and the gathering dusk made it even more grim. He paused to close the shutters behind him and continued on down. He stepped on to the muddy bank and quickly crossed the moat. He set out over the heathland then glanced back. He glimpsed the sentry, but the only real danger was if the assassin was also looking out; that would be the most cruel of coincidences.

Ralph continued on. When he reached the trees, he stopped and listened, drew his dagger and walked deeper into the spinney. This copse, he reflected, must be very old; it contained beech, copper, sycamore and, of course, the great oak trees. He studied them closely. Which tree housed the treasure? An old forester had once told him that oaks could grow and survive for hundreds and hundreds of years, and they changed as they grew. Their great trunks split, branches became twisted and extended, they were damaged by thunder-storms and lightning.

'Think!' Ralph whispered. 'You are coming from a battle. You have something precious to hide.' Cerdic would have been in a hurry, eager to get back to the battlefield. So, what did he do? Dig?

Ralph smiled to himself. Cerdic would scarcely do that. He wouldn't have the time, energy or the tools to dig a deep hole. And anything hidden beneath the soil would soon be disturbed and discovered. Ralph gazed round, and counted seven great oak trees in all, interspersed by bushes and other trees. Wasn't seven a sacred number to the ancient rituals as well as to the Christian faith? Seven sacraments. Seven days of the week. Ralph got up and walked round the trees. He tried to put himself into the position of that bedraggled, weary, blood-spattered squire, a man entrusted with a sacred task.

Ralph stopped. The spinney was now very quiet as if the birds and animals who lived here resented his intrusion and quietly watched from the gathering shadows. He was standing before one of the ancient oak trees and looked up. He began to climb. At first it was difficult. He bruised his legs, scraped his hands but, at last, he reached the lower branches which provided him with a better foothold. Up and up he climbed till the branches thinned. He stared down the length of the great trunk. He could see no crack or rent, no gap or hole. He was about to climb down when he heard the murmur of voices and froze. Two men had entered the spinney from the other end. They were hooded and masked, quivers slung across their backs, bows in their hands. Poachers? Outlaws? The men stopped beneath him, whispering, their heads together. He could make out no face, no distinguishing mark. They crossed the glade and disappeared into the undergrowth. Ralph's arms ached. He was about to clamber down when three more abruptly appeared, following their companions across the glade. Ralph tried to make himself as comfortable as possible, grateful for the branches and leaves which concealed him. He waited and, eventually, the men came back, this time together in a group of five. Ralph peered down. They were certainly not from the castle and they did not seem intent on hunting game. They appeared to have simply gone to the fringe of the spinney, stared out at the castle then returned.

They must be from the village, Ralph thought. He waited until the men were gone then clambered down. Brythnoth's cross would have to wait. He ran across the clearing, out of the spinney and back towards the castle. He found Adam in the barbican talking to one of the guards.

'In Heaven's name, Ralph, what's the matter?'

'I don't know,' Ralph replied wiping the sweat from his face. 'I went out for a walk and . . .' He shook his head. 'I wish Sir John would listen. There's villainy being plotted in Maldon. Where is the Constable now?'

Adam shrugged. 'In his chambers, I think. Can I help?'

Ralph nodded. 'Sir John may listen to you. Tell him I've seen villagers armed with bows and arrows studying the castle. I urge him to double the guard. Put every man we have on a war footing.'

'Dramatic language, Ralph!'

'For the love of God, Adam, just do what I say! I'm going to check the Salt Tower.'

Adam hastened away. Ralph was pleased to be free of his questioning stare; he was also embarrassed by his own hypocrisy. Here he was urging his Constable to prepare the castle carefully and yet he had left that window door unsecured. He hurried to the Salt Tower and up the steps. The chamber was now very dark. The shutters, slightly opened by the evening breeze, allowed in some light. Ralph hurried across, pulled the shutters together and lowered the bar. He turned and sat, his back to the wall, trying to catch his breath. He was soaked in sweat. He got up and, as he did so, once again caught that pleasing fragrance Beatrice always wore.

'Are you there?' he whispered. 'Are you really near me?' Ralph felt a shiver go up his spine. He'd always believed that when a person died, the soul left the body and travelled on. Yet what had Father Aylred once told him? That some souls lingered in a twilight world between life and death? Was that happening now? Had Beatrice, who loved him so passionately, refused to journey on? Was she here with him now? Tears pricked his eyes. What did it matter whether or not he found Brythnoth's cross? The real treasure in his life had gone. And what should he do when all this was over? In his heart he knew he could not stay at Ravenscroft. It would always evoke memories of Beatrice and he could not live with that. For the moment, however, he had to stay because of the assassin who stalked them all; he could not leave the garrison in its moment of danger. But if he survived? If God brought him safely through this? Where to then? To the Halls of Oxford, to resume his studies of the great Aristotle? Ralph drew a deep breath. The tinge of perfume was even stronger. He remembered that Theobald had distilled it. Ralph chewed on his lip. He'd ask the physician for one last jar, a keepsake.

Ralph walked to the door. He thought of the upper chamber from which the assassin had loosed his killing shaft and went up the crumbling steps, ignoring the squeak of rats as they scampered away. The upper room was colder than when he had last visited it, the shutters had not been fully closed. He went and looked out of a window. It was almost night and a mist was creeping in from Devil's Spinney, curling out towards the castle. Father Aylred would be waiting for him. Castle servants had already laid out the altar, cross and sacred vessels. Sir John had agreed that Ralph could act as altar boy but no one else should be present.

Ralph walked back to the door and heard a sound on the stairs. A rat? He took out his dagger, gripping it firmly because his hands were sweaty. With his back to the wall he went carefully down the steps. Again the sound. He turned a corner and listened. Was there someone there? Ralph could hear the beat of his own heart. He wished he had brought a candle. Had someone seen him come here? He swallowed hard. The tower steps were freezing. He could not stay here. He went on down. Suddenly his heel slipped, the dagger clattered on the steps. Cursing softly, Ralph crouched down and stretched out, and as he did so, his hand caught a piece of twine, tight like that of a drawn bow. He followed it across to some nails that had been driven into the wall from the time when the stairs had had a wooden rail or panelling. Each end of the twine was tied to one of these nails. Ralph lowered his hands. Another stretch of twine was there, just as taut, spanning a lower step. Ralph slashed through the twine with his dagger. He went down at a crouch, feeling rather ridiculous, as if he was a child learning to go up or down steps for the first time. He reached the bottom and fled from the Salt Tower.

He paused beneath a tree, re-sheathed his dagger and wiped the sweat from his face.

'God help you, Ralph!' he whispered. 'You are a fool, for all your logic!'

He had nearly fallen for one of the oldest tricks employed in the defence of a castle. Stone spiral staircases were dangerous at the best of times. On any other occasion he would have gone clattering down the steps. He would have tripped and the least he could have suffered was broken limbs; more probably he would have smashed his skull or snapped his neck. Someone had seen him go into the tower and immediately followed. It would be easy enough to take twine from an arbalest or bow and wrap it round those nails. Then it would only be a matter of waiting. He had had a lucky escape. Or was it luck? Was Beatrice here, guiding and protecting his every step? If the heel of his boot hadn't slipped, if he hadn't dropped the dagger . . . Ralph shivered at the thought. But who? Rage replaced his fear as he strode back towards the keep.

Sir John and Adam were standing on the green, heads together. The captain of the guard hovered nearby. Torches, lashed to poles, had been thrust into the ground. The Constable looked expectantly at him.

'Ralph, where have you been?'

He bit back an angry reply. 'Sir John, I'm more interested in where everybody else has been.'

Adam looked puzzled. 'What is the matter?'

'Adam and I have been together since we saw you walk across the green,' Sir John said brusquely.

'Did you see anyone else go towards the Salt Tower?'

'No.' Adam shook his head. 'Why, Ralph, what has happened?'

'Nothing, nothing at all.' Ralph sighed. 'Look, Sir John, this castle is vulnerable, the Salt Tower is not securely guarded. That large window door should be bricked up.'

'Ralph, Ralph, calm yourself. I know dreadful things are happening. Adam here says that you think we are in some danger. But from whom? How could a group of ragged-arsed peasants take a castle like this?'

'What happens if there is a rebel army in the vicinity?' Ralph replied heatedly. 'Sir John, you fought the French. The men who throng the Pot of Thyme in Maldon are the sons of those who brought down the cream of French chivalry at Crécy and Poitiers.'

'I've doubled the guards. I'll see to the Salt Tower.' Sir John looked towards the main gate. 'I'll be glad when the royal commissioners arrive. They'll advise me.' And he walked off, shaking his head.

'He's tired,' Ralph said quietly. 'He's an old and rather frightened man.'

'Be gentle in your judgements, Ralph,' Adam replied. 'Sir John is a warrior; he mounts his horse and charges the enemy. He's not skilled in dealing with secret assassins and prowling outlaws.' Adam took a step closer, his handsome face full of concern. 'I don't like this place, Ralph. Forget Brythnoth's treasure. Let's be away from it. We could pile our possessions on to a sumpter pony and be gone. Clerks like ourselves will always find comfortable benefices, good employment.'

Ralph was about to reply when he heard his name being called. Father Aylred was beckoning him over.

'I must go.' And, making his apologies, Ralph hurried over to the priest.

Father Aylred looked tired and anxious. He plucked at Ralph's sleeve and took him into the tower, locking and bolting the door behind him.

'All is ready,' he said. 'Sir John has cleared Midnight Tower of everyone.'

Ralph gazed around. The vestibule had been transformed. All the sconce torches had been lit and burnt fiercely against the darkness. At the bottom of the steps a small altar had been set up, covered with a linen cloth. On this stood candles, a small metal cross, a wooden triptych, breviary, chalice and paten with two offertory cruets, one full of wine, the other of water. On a small stool lay the black and gold vestments for a Requiem Mass. On the wall above, a makeshift crucifix had been fixed.

'We should begin now,' Father Aylred said wearily. 'The sooner the better.'

'Are you well enough, Father? It can always wait. Do you think this is really necessary?'

'The dead are close about us here,' the priest replied hoarsely. He rubbed the side of his head. 'They throng about. There's wickedness, an evil which has to be purged, sins that cry out to be forgiven. The Mass for the dead will provide some light and hallow this dreadful place.'

Ralph forgot his own misgivings and helped the priest dress. Then Father Aylred stood at the altar. He bowed and kissed the red cross painted in the centre of the altar cloth.

'*In nomine Patris et Filii et Spiritus Sancti* . . . I will go unto the altar of God,' he intoned, 'to the God who gives joy to my youth.'

Ralph was about to reply when another voice spoke, clear as a bell.

'I will go unto the altar of God, to the God who gives joy to my youth!'

Both priest and clerk froze. The voice was not pleasant, mocking in its imitation.

'We should leave this,' Ralph urged.

'That's right, clerk, piss off!' the voice snapped.

Two of the candles went out.

'Why don't both of you just piss off and leave us alone? What good is this mummery!'

Father Aylred calmly crossed himself again and began the Mass. This time there were no offensive remarks. Ralph nervously glanced up. The flames of the sconce torches had changed; they were no longer red and vigorous but weak with a bluish tinge. He noticed how cold it had grown and there was an offensive stench as if a cesspit had been opened. Father Aylred remained resolute. He opened the missal and quietly recited the collect, followed by the epistle. He was about to move the missal to the right side of the altar for the gospel when one of the sconce torches fell from its bracket, narrowly missing the altar, to clatter on to the floor.

'Look, Ralph!' the voice commanded. 'Look up the stair-well!'

He obeyed and sprang back in horror. The darkened stair-well had disappeared. He stood at the mouth of a heavily wooded valley. He was sure a veritable army was hidden among the trees on either side. Along the floor of the valley a man leading a sumpter pony was coming towards him. At every step the bells sewn on his jerkin jingled; it was as if some madcap child had seized a cluster of handbells and was ringing them for the sheer malicious joy of shattering the silence.

'Don't look!' Father Aylred whispered over his shoulder. 'Ralph, the Gospel according to St Mark.'

Ralph tore his eyes away and stared at the gold cross on

the back of the priest's chasuble. He forced himself to make the sign on his forehead, lips and heart, a symbolic gesture indicating that he was prepared to listen to and act on the gospel reading. The tower fell silent. Father Aylred finished the reading and moved to the offertory. The bread and wine were raised. Ralph, as if in a dream, got up to help him prepare the lavabo, where the priest washes his hands before the consecration.

Aylred's face was now soaked in sweat. 'Remember the Mass, Ralph,' he whispered. 'Try not to let the darkness daunt you. Say the psalm with me.'

'I will wash my hands among the innocent, I will encompass thine altar, Oh Lord, that I may hear the song of your praise and tell them all of your wondrous work.'

'You stupid bastards!'

Ralph was sure the voice was Beardsmore's.

'Ralph, you are a clerk! Tell this hedge-priest he's just farting in the wind!'

The door to the tower started to shake as if mailed men were trying to break through. The same sound came from the stairs behind as if a horde of marauders had broken in and were clattering down, swords at the ready. Aylred grasped Ralph's wrists and kept him at the altar.

'Stay here!' he whispered. 'Stay with me!'

Ralph was too frightened to move. A cacophony of sound broke out. People shouting, crying, moaning, accompanied by pungent, acrid smells. Faces appeared on the walls as if the stonework was being sculpted by invisible hands.

Somewhere a wolf howled. Ralph looked up. The wall opposite had disappeared. He was in that valley again. The eerie figure was moving towards him. Two great mastiffs had appeared with eyes like hell's fire, cruel teeth bared. Ralph felt something kick his ankle and stared down at the priest who held the Host in his hands.

'Stay next to me, Ralph, and watch what I hold.'

Ralph obeyed. The phenomena around him became more intense. Both men had to brace themselves against a rushing wind which seemed to come through the walls. Ralph felt as if he was on the prow of a ship heading into a storm. Shapes and shadows flitted round the altar. Father Aylred was quiet now, weak, but the sacred words were uttered. The bread and wine became the sacred Body of Christ. Everything fell silent. Father Aylred intoned the prayer for the dead, the solemn invocation that Christ and his angels would take all the souls of the faithful to a place of calm and peace. After that the disturbance faded. The sconce torches burnt more fiercely. But, just when Ralph thought they would be troubled no further, he felt as if doors were slamming shut around the altar, trapping them in a cage. Ralph was seized by a great terror as if some hideous horror from Hell was standing close by. A deep despair swept over him, a sense that all this was futile, a waste of time, and when the voice spoke, it seemed to come from the depths of his own heart.

'What's the use, Ralph? What is the bloody use of all this? Where's Beatrice?' A pause. 'You know where she is!

Wandering the snowy wastelands of Hell. Leave this priest to his mumblings.'

'No, she isn't!' Father Aylred suddenly exclaimed. He turned his pallid, sweat-soaked face to Ralph. 'My mother's in Heaven,' he gasped. 'Isn't she, Ralph?'

The clerk opened his mouth.

'I've wasted my life. I might as well whistle across the graveyard. It's so futile.'

'It's not futile!' Ralph found it difficult to speak. 'It's not futile at all, Father!'

The priest looked as if he was going to leave the altar. He placed the Host down and stood, slightly swaying, as if he wanted to walk away but could not.

'Take him away!' the voice urged Ralph. 'What he needs is a good cup of claret and a warm pair of tits!'

'Let's be away,' Father Aylred hissed. 'I say Mass and God doesn't listen!'

A chorus swelled up, demonic voices shouting, 'Go! Go!' The rattling on the stairs, an icy coldness. Ralph realised that Aylred had reached the doxology of the Mass. He stretched out and picked up the chalice and the sacred Host. They both felt hot to the touch.

'Say the words!' he whispered.

Aylred swayed, face white, eyes dark pools of anguish.

'Say the words!' Ralph insisted.

Aylred turned away to retch. He leaned against the wall, spluttering and coughing. He began to edge towards the door. Ralph seized him and brought him back. He thrust him against the altar, eyes on the Host and chalice, ignoring the nagging insistence of the voice within. Ralph grasped the chalice and Host.

'Say the words!'

'*Per Ipsum, in Ipso, et cum Ipso*. Through Him, in Him and with Him . . .' intoned Father Aylred.

Ralph lifted the Host above the chalice.

'All honour and glory and power are yours, Oh Heavenly Father!'

Ralph suddenly felt warm and relaxed. One, two then three spheres of light appeared as if from nowhere, like the brilliant flames of glowing beeswax candles. The sensation of being shut in disappeared. A warm fragrance rose up from the altar. Aylred sighed and continued with the Mass. The Our Father, the Kiss of Peace, the Communion; in the end all was peaceful. Ralph had to help Father Aylred to a stool.

'What happened there?' he asked.

'Can't you feel it, Ralph?'

'Are you well, Father?'

'Can't you feel it?' the Franciscan repeated. 'So warm, so peaceful.'

'Yes,' said Ralph. 'I can feel it.'

'When I was younger and more handsome,' Father Aylred smiled, 'I was an exorcist. This is not the first time I've confronted demons.'

'So you are not the hedge-priest you pretend to be?'

The Franciscan blinked. 'Once, Ralph, I lectured in the Halls of Oxford. I was arrogant, so full of myself I had no room for God. I was a demon-hunter. One day I was called to an exorcism, a young woman in Binsey. I didn't prepare myself well. The exorcism went wrong and the young woman died.' He glanced up. 'But I've been doing penance ever since. I pray to St Thomas à Becket. You know how our order has a great devotion to him. I would love to go on pilgrimage to his shrine, Ralph, but I'm too weak, too frail. Each year I promise, each year I fail. One year I must.' He wiped his eyes on the back of his hands. 'And if I don't, Ralph?'

'Oh, you will.' Ralph smiled. 'And I'll go with you.'

Father Aylred shook his head. 'I learnt a secret tonight, Ralph. I'll come through this. But, before Christmas, I am going to die. I must prepare for the long journey I have to make.' He got up and began to divest, laying out the robes. He swayed on his feet but Ralph caught him.

'Come on, Father. I'll take you back to your chamber. We'll share a cup of wine.'

Chapter 3

Beatrice had watched the soul-catching drama which unfolded in the stairwell of Midnight Tower. All the shades and phantasms she had glimpsed in Ravenscroft assembled there: Black Malkyn, Lady Johanna, Crispin and Clothilde, other shades and shapes and, standing near the door, the Minstrel Man.

Beatrice felt as if all reality was on the verge of crumbling, like it had when she had fallen from the parapet. At times the tower disappeared and the altar stood in a snow-covered field fringed by dark, threatening forests or a red sandy waste where a hot wind blasted all forms of terrors around the altar.

She could see that Father Aylred was weakening though Ralph stood his ground. Black Malkyn and Lady Johanna screamed. Other ghouls gathered, bathing the altar in their fetid breath, running up and down the steps in a clatter of feet and a rattle of weapons. All the time the Minstrel Man watched with hate-filled eyes as the priest celebrated the divine sacrifice. Beatrice found herself unable to help. She was torn between anxiety for Ralph and the sudden changes

195

of vista and landscape. They were in the field again. Father Aylred was bracing himself against freezing gusts of wind. Mailed horsemen left the forest and charged, lances levelled, at both priest and clerk. Beatrice stared around. This was the Mass surely. Someone would help.

The Minstrel Man appeared to be drawing closer. He seemed unaware of the other phantasms, eyes intent on the priest. Beatrice had never seen such malice, such a tangible hatred. She could almost stretch out and touch his desire to kill. As Father Aylred began the consecration, the Minstrel Man lifted his hands, talking in a gibberish tongue to the darkness around him. A silver disc of light appeared but then vanished. They were on a lake, the altar was in the centre, the water was frozen solid. Beatrice gazed in horror at the heads just above the ice, fastened tight, hair awry, mouths gaping, eyes staring. Then they were in that burning desert and all sorts of terrors seized her soul. Large feather-winged birds massed over the altar. Horsemen milled about on the far horizon. The earth cracked like a crust of bread and columns of fire appeared. Across the desert trooped a legion of the damned with sightless eyes and yawning mouths. Beside them carts rattled on iron-rimmed wheels. They bore makeshift scaffolds from which white-purplish cadavers danced in the final throes of death.

Beatrice moaned. She wanted to move from here, to go into the darkness, seal her eyes against such hideous horrors. She saw the look on Ralph's face, sensed his fear, the desperate sense of loneliness. Yet, also, his firm courage to continue.

Now and again there were moments of peace: the tower disappeared and she glimpsed a hill with three crosses on top, soaring shapes against a setting sun, or Elizabeth Lockyer smiling at her. A group of children, happy and contented, unaware of the terrors, clustered together smiling up at the priest and Ralph as if fascinated by what they were doing.

The Minstrel Man drew closer to the altar. He was reciting a mocking echo of Father Aylred's words. Beatrice recognised the issue at hand. The Minstrel Man had released hideous images but they were harmless enough. They could do little except weaken the resolve of the priest, make him give up and flee this place. He'd thereby acknowledge, by his lack of faith, the supremacy of this demon lord who'd swept up from Hell.

Sheets of molten metal appeared as if from nowhere, screening off the altar, boxing both priest and clerk inside. They were transparent but gave off a power which repelled Beatrice. It seemed as if both Father Aylred and the man she loved had been trapped in some hideous cell fashioned by Hell. The reason was simple. Aylred's faith was failing. Beatrice recalled her encounter with the Moon people on the road. She moved closer to the altar, willing the priest to continue but Father Aylred was unreceptive. He moved away, going towards the wall to retch and vomit. Beatrice turned her attention to Ralph, willing with all her soul that he stand his ground.

The Minstrel Man drew closer. A look of triumph played on his lips. The other phantasms he had summoned up, the hideous, repellent shapes, appeared outside the cage he had formed.

Again the tower disappeared. They were now in the hall of some castle. All around was a brooding darkness, broken only by flickering red candles. For the first time since her fall from the parapet, Beatrice experienced true terror, a soul-crushing sensation of despondency and despair.

'Pray, Beatrice Arrowner!' Brother Antony was kneeling beside her. She fell to her knees, hands clasped.

'This is the Mass,' she hissed. 'The sacrifice of God's own Son!'

'Pray,' Brother Antony repeated. 'It depends on man's faith.'

She obeyed and, when she looked up, they were back in the vestibule of the Midnight Tower. Ralph was forcing the chalice into Father Aylred's hands. The priest began the words of the solemn doxology. Abruptly there was a change. Other presences made themselves felt, expressed in columns of white-hot light grouped around the altar. The chalice was raised, it seemed to hover by itself in the air. The wine was bubbling to the top and from it shot fire, scarlet flames drenching the altar. Golden spheres appeared. The cage disappeared. The Minstrel Man, the leering faces of Crispin and Clothilde abruptly vanished. All that remained was a musty little stairwell and a sweat-soaked priest finishing the Mass.

'It's over.' Brother Antony went up the stairs, smiling over his shoulder. 'Soon, Beatrice, it will all be over.'

Beatrice watched Ralph consoling and comforting the old priest. She, too, acknowledged a change: that light, the fire she had seen from the chalice – she wanted to be with it. She was tired. The spiritual contest had drained her. She wanted to travel on. This world of shadows and fleeting shapes was unreal.

Ralph was now helping the priest towards the door. Beatrice glanced at the stairwell. If only Brother Antony had stayed.

Ralph took Father Aylred to his chamber. The castle was deserted apart from the sentries on the parapet walk and the occasional sleepy-eyed scullion taking up food or drink to those doing the night watch. At first Father Aylred kept his own counsel, as if his short speech after Mass had exhausted him. Ralph had his hand on the latch of his chamber when Father Aylred shook his head.

'Take me downstairs, Ralph. Let me at least go to the chapel and give thanks.'

'We've prayed enough,' Ralph said lightly. 'The good Lord will understand.'

'I want to be there.' The priest's voice was almost petulant. 'I should also go back and collect my robes.'

'I will do that,' Ralph reassured him. 'But come, if you want to go to the chapel.'

He took the priest back down the steps. The chapel was in darkness. Ralph used a tinder to light some candles and the torches in both the sanctuary and nave. Father Aylred sat on a stool just inside the rood screen staring at the altar. Ralph sat on the other side; he felt tired, hungry and thirsty, but the priest needed both comfort and company. Ralph closed his eyes and said his own prayer for guidance. He began to doze so got up to stretch his legs. To keep himself awake he studied the wall paintings. On the left of the altar the artist had depicted the seven days of Creation. Each day had a Roman numeral, and on each panel the artist had also portrayed a scene from Christ's passion and death. Ralph stopped and studied the one beneath the Roman numeral V: the Old Testament scene didn't concern him but the one from the Gospels caught his attention. Christ nailed to a tree, behind him a dark, threatening forest. Ralph felt his stomach pitch.

'On an altar to your God and mine,' he whispered. The fifth oak tree! But from the left or the right? Ralph clenched his hands in excitement. Tomorrow morning he would see which, he would find Brythnoth's cross!

'Ralph, could you take me up now?' Aylred was staring sleepily at him.

'Of course, Father.'

He extinguished the lights and helped the old priest up the spiral staircase. At the top, Father Aylred turned and shook his hand.

'Thank you, Ralph. If you could just go back to Midnight Tower and collect my robes?'

Ralph went down the steps and out. The night sky was brilliant with stars, the breeze refreshing. He walked towards Midnight Tower but then decided against returning immediately to that place. He wanted to savour ordinary things: grass trees, the smell of the earth. He was also haunted by memories of Beatrice. How they would walk out on a night like this and sit on the green or beneath one of the trees in the orchard. They'd talk and talk about the future. They often left it far too late and he would have to accompany her back to the barbican and down the road into Maldon. Ralph blinked away the tears. He was on the edge of the overgrown garden which led to the small orchard below the Salt Tower. The full realisation of what he had experienced during the Mass suddenly swept over him. There was a world other than his and it was only a step away. Beatrice was in that world.

Ralph stopped under one of the trees and sat down, his back against the trunk. In the poor light he could just make out the outlines of the Salt Tower and the overgrown grass and gorse that fringed the door. He was distracted. In a way he couldn't explain, the Mass had been a turning point. He had lost Beatrice. She would never return and he must leave Ravenscroft. So strong was his desire that he almost felt like going to his chamber and packing his possessions there and them. He'd seek an interview with Sir John Grasse and, at first light, he'd be gone. But the Constable would miss him, and such actions might provoke suspicions. Ralph chewed on his lip. Until the assassin was caught, he, like the others, lay under suspicion.

Ralph glanced up at the Salt Tower and then froze. He was sure he had seen it! A pinprick of light from one of the unshuttered windows, as if someone was on the stairwell carrying a torch or candle. Was the assassin there now? Was he preparing some fresh mischief? Ralph cursed. He had no war belt on, only a small dagger. He pulled it out and ran at a half-crouch. He quietly cursed as the briars caught his legs. He reached the door to the Salt Tower. It was unlocked. Surely Sir John had left a guard here. Hadn't he seen two archers go across just before Mass?

Ralph pulled the door open and stepped inside, standing silently in the musty darkness. At first he thought his eyes had played some trick, his imagination running riot. He was about to leave when he heard the clink of metal and the hiss of voices. There were more than one in the Tower, he could almost feel them clustered further up the stairwell. He remembered Devil's Spinney, those cloaked, cowled men with their bows and quivers. Ravenscroft was under attack! The rebels had stolen across the heathland and into the tower. The two archers must have been killed.

Ralph left the tower. Instead of running through the orchard, he kept to the line of the wall and almost tripped over the body of a guard. He crouched down. There had been two sentries on the parapet walk either side of the Salt Tower. This one was dead. Despite the darkness, some skilled archer had sent a yew shaft straight through his chest. Ralph delayed no longer but sped back towards the keep, shouting and yelling. A soldier loomed out of the darkness. Ralph recognised the captain of the watch.

'We are under attack!' he screamed.

The captain of the guard ran back to where the alarm horn hung on a post in the bailey. He grasped it and blew. The horn was clogged. Ralph looked over his shoulder: a dark shape was slipping through the trees. The captain of the guard spat, cleared the horn and, this time, blew a long, wailing blast. Sentries from the parapet had already noticed something was amiss and were hastening down the steps. The captain of the guard ran and shoved Ralph aside. He fell to the grass. He heard the clash of swords – the intruders had already reached the castle green and the captain's swift action had saved Ralph. He crawled away. His saviour was facing two opponents. Ralph drew his dagger and ran. He felt his head butt into a soft stomach as he lashed out with the dagger. Hot blood spattered on his hands, the cowled assailant fell away. The captain of the guard drove off the other attacker and, grasping Ralph by the arm, pulled him away.

The men-at-arms were already forming up according to the drill they had been taught. Some were not properly clothed, roused from their beds, but they had donned helmets and brought along shields and lances. Behind these, archers were forming up. Sergeants were yelling orders. An arrow whipped through the darkness and took one of the castle garrison in the face. The man dropped his shield and turned away, screaming in agony. The shield wall formed more tightly. Sir John Grasse appeared. Guards were despatched to secure entrances and doorways. The attackers hung back. Apart from the two who had made their lightning attack on the captain, the rest were uncertain. They had expected to find a sleepy garrison, seize the keep, perhaps take Sir John prisoner, but Ralph's alarm, as well as their own fear and inexperience, made them hesitate.

They lurked among the trees on the far side of the keep. The night air was rent by screams as sentries on the parapet walls shot into the trees, finding their targets. Sir John, wearing a ridiculous-looking tilting helm, lifted the visor and raised his sword.

'Right, lads, advance!'

Ralph grasped the shield and lance dropped by the wounded man-at-arms. The garrison moved carefully across the green and round the keep. At Sir John's order they stopped. A few attackers came forward. Sir John had had the foresight to have sconce torches thrown on the grass to provide some light. The archers behind the men-at-arms took aim, arrows whirred through the air and caught the intruders, sending them spinning, coughing and choking back into the darkness. Ralph knew the attack was over. It had been led by hotheads, they had counted on surprise and been thwarted. Now they were terrified of being cut off from the Salt Tower, their only means of escape. Nevertheless, Sir John moved cautiously. A horn sounded from the darkness and the intruders fled. Sir John would have ordered a full pursuit but Ralph grasped him by the arm.

'Don't!' he said. 'Let them go. They'll only fortify the Salt Tower and wreak havoc on our attack.'

Sir John agreed. The troops were ordered to pause and they stood, sweating, chests heaving, peering into the darkness. Adam appeared, sword belt clasped round him. Sir John told him to take a few archers forward, and they flitted into the trees. The occasional scream followed their departure.

'The archers must be finishing off the wounded,' Sir John growled. 'It's just as well and saves us a few hangings.'

Adam appeared, a smile on his face, the blade of his sword bloody.

'Sir John, Master Ralph, they have gone. Fleeing across the heath back into Devil's Spinney.'

The Constable told his men to stand at ease. Followed by Ralph and his archers, he crossed the overgrown orchard and garden. Here and there a corpse sprawled in a pool of spreading blood, eyes open, mouths gaping.

'There are no wounded,' Adam remarked. 'It will teach them a lesson.'

Ralph hid a tremor of unease: killing when the blood was hot, in battle, sword against sword, he understood but this callous slaughter of injured men turned his stomach. Sir John, however, had no qualms. He turned one or two corpses over and roared at an archer to bring a torch. He then scrutinised the bodies.

'Thanks be to God,' he muttered. 'They are not local men.'

'But there must have been people from Maldon among them,' Adam declared. 'To lead them across the moat and down to . . .'

Sir John got up, took off his helmet and threw it on the ground. 'It's like wearing a chamber pot!' he cursed. 'Those men could be outlaws, or rebels who have moved south looking for a fight, stirring up the local people. Get Father Aylred,' he called out to an archer. 'And Vavasour. Rouse them now!'

They went into the Salt Tower. In the light of the sconce torch, Ralph saw bloodstains on the steps where the attackers had dragged away their wounded. In the room which contained the large door window lay the corpses of the two archers who had been on guard duty here. The shutters were open. Ralph grasped a torch and stared out into the darkness. He could see the makeshift bridge the attackers had thrown over the moat. Across the heathland the cold night wind stirred the grass, the silence broken only by the haunting call of some animal on the prowl.

He went to close the shutters and became aware of pain in his right hand. He had an ugly gash across his knuckles.

'You should get that dressed.' Sir John came forward. 'Ask Theobald Vavasour to take a look.'

Adam accompanied him out of the Salt Tower. The physician and Father Aylred were already moving among the corpses.

'It's nothing,' Ralph whispered. 'I can dress it myself.'

'Nonsense.' Adam seized him by the arm. 'Marisa can do it. She's up anyway and she'll want to know the news.'

Ravenscroft was now bustling. Women and children came out to see what had happened as Adam led Ralph across into Midnight Tower.

The altar still stood there, the chalice and paten on a chair, the altar cloths neatly piled.

'What happened?' Adam asked.

'Oh, Father Aylred thinks the place is haunted.'

Ralph was more aware of how painful his hand had become.

'He celebrated a Mass.'

'And what happened?'

'Nothing, nothing at all. Adam, I am sorry, but my hand hurts.'

Ralph followed Adam up the steps.

Marisa was waiting in their chamber: a large, oval-shaped room, comfortably furnished. Cloths and tapestries hung on the walls. In the centre was a large four-poster bed with blue and gold fringed curtains neatly tied back, the bolsters white and crisp. Everything was neat and tidy. Two braziers stood in the centre of the room. Beneath their metal caps the charcoal spluttered and sparked on the fragrant herbs Marisa had sprinkled there. She was sitting in the window seat clutching a dagger.

'Don't be foolish,' her husband laughed. 'The attack is over.'

Marisa threw the dagger down and raced across the room, wrapping her arms round Adam's neck. She forgot all modesty and kissed him full on the lips.

Adam gently extricated himself. 'If it hadn't been for Ralph the castle would have been overrun. His hand is cut.'

Marisa immediately tended to it, telling her husband to fill the water bowl from the lavarium. She made Ralph sit on the edge of the bed and cleaned the wound with a rag.

'It's not too deep,' she said. 'Adam, bring me some of the salve Theobald gave us. I don't know what is in this.' Marisa gently rubbed the grease on the cut, making it smart. 'But it will keep the wound from festering.' Helped by

Adam, she took a piece of linen and bound the wound carefully.

Ralph felt self-conscious. This was the nearest he had been to any woman since Beatrice had died. He could smell the perfume Beatrice had worn and he remembered he had given it all to Marisa shortly after Beatrice's death.

'You should rest, Ralph.'

Ralph stared across the chamber. On a small table beneath the crucifix were other jars of unguents and creams. Marisa followed his gaze.

'I am sorry, Ralph,' she whispered. 'They must bring back memories.'

'No, no, I'm glad I gave them to you.' He grinned at Adam. 'You are a very lucky man.'

'And you are a very sad one.'

Ralph shrugged. 'But not for long.'

'Why is that?'

'I'll be gone soon.' Ralph lifted his bandaged hand. 'And don't take offence, Adam, but I'll be going alone. Ravenscroft has too many memories. It's like being pricked time and again by a dagger.' He got to his feet.

'And Brythnoth's cross?' Adam asked.

Ralph shrugged. 'I'll give you the manuscripts. You find it.'

'Where will you go?'

'Cambridge or Oxford.' Ralph thanked Marisa, bade them good night and left.

He found Father Aylred in the vestibule collecting the chalice paten and altar cloths. The priest looked more composed though he was still white-faced with dark rings under his eyes.

'A sad night, eh, Ralph? Such foolishness. So many souls sent unshriven into the darkness.'

'How many were killed?' Ralph asked.

'Five of the garrison and eleven assailants. One was in the moat, apparently too wounded for his friends to carry. The poor man died like a dog.' He saw the bandage on Ralph's hand. 'Are you hurt?'

'Just a cut, Father. Do you need any help?'

The priest shook his head. 'No, there'll not be much sleep tonight at Ravenscroft and these cannot stay here. You are going to leave, aren't you, Ralph?'

'Yes, Father, I am, as soon as I can. I think Sir John will release me from my indentures.'

'It's well that you go, Ralph. There's terrible evil here.'

'Who brought it, Father?'

'I don't know.' The priest sat down on the bench, placing the altar cloths in his lap. 'Ravenscroft, until recently, was a quiet, happy place.' He waved his hand. 'True, this place was supposed to be haunted. But in a castle as old as Ravenscroft I suppose there'll always be unquiet spirits.'

'So what happened here during Mass?' Ralph asked curiously.

'I don't know. But I can hazard a guess. There's human weakness and misery, but real malice, planned evil is something different. It calls up the Lords of Hell. That's what I felt. Not just the unquiet and troubled souls which may still lurk in the shadows but a real malignant presence. I ask myself, what would bring that here?'

'And what answer did you get?'

'Like is attracted to like, Ralph. One of us in this castle, as you know, has become a killer. Such evil would attract the attention of Hell.' He sketched a blessing. 'What happened tonight is nothing to what might be planned. Tread carefully!'

Ralph went out across to the Lion Tower and climbed to his own room. He unlocked the door and went in. He lay down on the bed and stared up at the ceiling, recalling the night's events and Father Aylred's sombre words. He looked at the bandage on his hand and smiled, sniffed at it and then gasped. He sat up, swinging his legs off the bed. Other words, scraps of conversation came jumbling back. Ralph felt the sweat break out on his skin. No, it couldn't be. He forgot his sore hand and went across to the table. Smoothing a piece of parchment, he listed the victims, those who had been killed since this terrible business had begun. For a while he studied it then, throwing his quill down, Ralph put his face in his hands and wept softly.

Chapter 4

Beatrice was alarmed. The fall from the parapet had shattered one world, now the Mass in Midnight Tower was causing further changes. The strange coppery light was strengthening to a fiery glow. The silver discs were more radiant. The sky had turned a strange blue-gold colour, and the golden spheres were ever present in and around Ravenscroft. She herself felt stronger. She despised Crispin and Clothilde whom she glimpsed with the Minstrel Man in different parts of the castle. They were now subdued, plotting among themselves. Black Malkyn was calmer, while Lady Johanna had disappeared. No more did she haunt and wail in the cellar beneath Midnight Tower.

'She has travelled on,' Brother Antony explained as they stood on the green after the Mass.

'Why?' Beatrice asked.

'She wanted to let go. She broke free from her prison and is now allowed to travel on.'

'And these shapes and shades? Will they always remain?'

Brother Antony shook his head. 'As time goes by the will grow fainter, like echoes in a room, before disappearing altogether.'

'And what about the others? Black Malkyn. That unfortunate at the crossroads.'

'Slowly, surely their wills will edge towards a conclusion So when they want to, their journey will begin.'

'And me?' Beatrice laughed. She glanced over her shoulde across the bailey. She wanted to make sure Ralph was well

'Only you can answer that, Beatrice Arrowner. What d you yourself want?'

Beatrice stared around. All the familiar sights were here, th tubs and buckets, the bench near the wall, its legs overgrow by weeds; the barbican, the road down to Maldon. Beatric guiltily remembered her aunt and uncle.

'I must go and see them,' she said.

'Why?' Brother Antony asked.

'I don't know. But I realise I must leave them.'

'And Ralph?'

'I shall always love him. Whatever journey I make, I shal always wait for him.'

Brother Antony smiled. 'And that is good, Beatrice. Whe Ralph begins his journey, the more you want him, the faste he will travel.'

'And where will we travel to?'

'You know that, Beatrice. To God, and God is eternal. Th journey will be marvellous. Do you want to go, Beatrice?'

'I want to say farewell.'

'Of course you do.'

'But why can't I help?'

'Since your death, Beatrice Arrowner, you have done great good.'

She stared, puzzled. The castle had disappeared. They were standing on the edge of a most beautiful valley. A brook gurgled, the sunlight danced, the air was thick with the fragrance of wild roses. Brother Antony touched her face. She was aware only of his eyes.

'What do you mean, I did good?'

'Elizabeth Lockyer,' he replied. 'The old beggar man out on the heath. The comfort you gave Etheldreda at the crossroads. The poor Moon people, even Goodman Winthrop. As you will in life, so in death, Beatrice. Before you travel, you shall receive your reward.'

Beatrice stamped her foot. 'Why can't I help Ralph now? I can travel where I wish. I can listen to conversations. I can find the assassin.'

'Could you, Beatrice? Could you really?' Brother Antony smiled. 'Can you enter someone else's soul and discover their dark designs? Do you not remember the Gospels? Only God sees the things done in secret. That does not mean justice is frustrated, it will be done.'

'Will it?' Beatrice asked.

'Oh yes. The Minstrel Man will know that justice is near. He has gone to Ravenscroft to collect his own.' Brother Antony walked away and disappeared.

'Beatrice! Beatrice!' Crispin and Clothilde were before

her, hands together, their angelic faces troubled and anxious. 'Don't you want to talk to us any more? Aren't we friends?'

'You are one and the same,' Beatrice replied. 'You do not wish me well.'

A strange whistling rent the air. The Minstrel Man was swaggering towards her, thumbs tucked in his belt. He moved slowly, like a cat ready to spring. His slightly slanted eyes were full of mockery. He stopped and sniffed the air like some hunting dog.

'Don't you smell it, Beatrice Arrowner? The iron tang of blood?'

'Leave me alone.' Beatrice stepped back. 'In God's name, leave me alone!'

Crispin and Clothilde separated. The Minstrel Man gave the most mocking bow.

'Then be on your way, Beatrice Arrowner, though the day is not yet finished.'

Beatrice hastened out along the trackway. The hedges and grass loomed dark against the coppery light. Figures flitted across the path and, when she turned, she was sure those two great hounds of the Minstrel Man were loping silently behind her. Sometimes her concentration failed. Visions and phantasms sprang up before her: stretches of desert; freezing lakes of ice; trees alight with fire; a low sky with stars that were bright and close. Strange voices spoke, whispers of conversation. Jagged lightning cracked and flashed above Devil's Spinney. Horsemen with flapping banners and billowing cloaks, rode by her

Beatrice stopped. The trackway had ended; beneath her was a raging inferno.

'I'm only young and weak,' Beatrice prayed. 'All I want is to see them just one more time.'

She looked again. The visions had disappeared and she was home. Aunt Catherine was baking bread. She had built up the fire to heat the ovens on either side and was now heaping the dough on spatulas of wood, ready to bake them. Uncle Robert was sitting at the table trying to mend a leather belt. Beatrice stood and relished the homely atmosphere. Uncle Robert mentioned her name. Aunt Catherine turned away, fighting back the tears. Uncle Robert got up, put his hand on his wife's shoulder and gently kissed the back of her head.

'I'll stay with you,' he said. 'I'll not go down to the Pot of Thyme tonight. Anyway, there's trouble brewing. They should leave Ravenscroft alone.'

Beatrice went up to Aunt Catherine, put her arms round her neck and kissed her on both cheeks as if she was going to bed. She then did the same to Uncle Robert. Beatrice willed with all her might that they'd remember how she loved them, that she was grateful for what they had done, that she'd never forget. Aunt Catherine dropped the cloth she held and staggered slightly. Uncle Robert caught her and made her sit down on a stool at the head of the table.

'What's the matter, my heart?' he asked. 'Don't you feel well?'

'You know what I felt,' her aunt replied quietly.

'Beatrice?'

She nodded. 'Oh, Robert, it was as if she was here, just for a few seconds. As if she had come back from the castle and was hurrying up to her chamber.'

Uncle Robert's eyes filled with tears. 'I felt the same.'

He glanced around but Beatrice was leaving, hastening down the high street towards the Pot of Thyme. One look in the long, shadow-filled garden which ran round the back of the tavern told her Uncle Robert was not being fanciful. The place was full of men and these were not local peasants. They had travelled far; they were dressed in weather-stained doublets with cowls and hoods pulled over their heads. Many of them were well armed with bows and arrows, swords, daggers, clubs, billhooks and hauberks. They carried a black banner tied to a pole. Beatrice recalled the stories from her former life. How the southern shires were full of secret armies, of landless peasants waiting to raise the black banner of revolt and storm the King's castles. An attack upon Ravenscroft must be imminent. But what could she do? How could she warn Ralph?

In a trice Beatrice was running out of Maldon, taking the trackway to Ravenscroft. She seemed to move as if in one of her dreams, her feet hardly touching the ground, carried forward by her own will and her deep anxiety for Ralph. The towers and turrets of Ravenscroft came into sight but the track was blocked by the Minstrel Man with his ghastly-looking sumpter pony and, on either side, Crispin and Clothilde standing so coyly. Beatrice tried to go round them but they moved with her, stopping her.

Why can't I go through? thought Beatrice. I am a spirit.

She moved into the field but they moved too. Beatrice recalled Brother Antony's words: 'As in life so in death'. She walked purposefully towards them.

'Out of my way!' she commanded.

'Why, Beatrice, we've only come to talk.' The Minstrel Man seemed taller, darker, more threatening.

'What are you going to do?' Beatrice mocked. 'Kill me?'

The Minstrel Man was staring at her. Now he had the face of a wolf. His eyes never left hers. She felt a blast of fiery heat which weakened her determination.

'Let me pass!'

'If you'd only stay awhile.' Clothilde came towards her, hips swaying. 'Ralph is in danger.'

'I know that! Get out of my way!'

'We can still help.' Crispin spoke. 'We can intervene.'

Clothilde picked up the refrain. 'We can intervene and save him. We know the great danger which threatens Ravenscroft, both from within and without.'

Beatrice was certain that whatever these offered would be wrong. She was weary of their games and tricks.

'Where are Robin and Isabella?' she taunted. 'Or have you tired of them?'

The Minstrel Man clicked his tongue in disapproval. Beatrice took a step forward. A hot wind sprang up like sudden gale, pressing her back.

'Beatrice Arrowner!' Brother Antony was standing behind them. He held his hands out. 'Do you want to come forward?'

'I can't.' She kept her eyes on those of the Minstrel Ma
'But I want to come.'

The Minstrel Man glanced over his shoulder. He snarle
something at Brother Antony who replied in a tongue Beatric
couldn't understand.

'Let her go,' Brother Antony ordered.

The air was full of dancing lights. The Minstrel Man mac
a gesture as if wafting away some irritating flies but Beatric
walked forward. She was through them and in her haste
reach the castle she even ignored Brother Antony.

Darkness had fallen but Ralph was not in his chambe
Beatrice was aware of only one thought. He must be
danger, she had to help. She went to Midnight Towe
the scene of Father Aylred's Mass, but it was empty. Sl
became confused: the Mass had taken place at night b
when she'd been in Maldon, darkness hadn't fallen. W;
this strange world she lived in beginning to break up? Ha
time itself become disjointed, like numbers out of place
Beatrice walked to the Salt Tower and climbed up to th
second floor. She stared in horror. The chamber was fillin
with men coming quietly through the window door. Tw
archers lay dead on the ground, their souls had already gon
Beatrice fled the tower, across the overgrown garden to whe
Ralph was sitting beneath a tree. She tried desperately to spea
to him, to warn him of what was coming. She did not kno
whether it was her or mere chance but Ralph noticed a light
the tower. Beatrice watched the unfolding drama: the attacke
sallying out, Ralph's cry, the brave defence by the captain

the guard and the consequent slaughter. All the time Beatrice stayed close to Ralph as if, by her very presence, she could protect him from all hurt. She was aware of the screams of the dying, the silver discs, golden spheres, the wraiths and those ghostly soldiers, all gathering on the battleground to meet the souls of the fallen. But she had only one thought, the protection of Ralph. She was with him when he was taken to Adam and Marisa's chamber and when he threw his quill down and began to sob. She tried to comfort him, to understand what had happened but she could not. She had to accept the truth of Brother Antony's words. She could observe, she could react but she could not enter the heart and mind of even the man she loved so much.

The next morning Ralph dressed and went down to the hall to break his fast. Then he wrote a quick note and handed it to the captain of the guard drilling his men on the green outside the keep. The garrison were in good heart after their victory the previous night. The soldier looked puzzled but Ralph refused to answer his questions.

'Just give that to Sir John. Beg him, and I mean beg him, to do exactly what I have asked.'

Ralph went up into Midnight Tower. Adam and Marisa were already preparing for the day's work. Marisa was dressed; she said she intended to go into Maldon to see what was happening there.

'Is that safe?' Ralph asked. 'I'd much prefer you to come with me.'

'Where are you going?' Adam, sitting on the edge of the bed, paused in pulling his boots on.

'I want you to come to Devil's Spinney with me. Brythnoth's cross is there.'

Both Adam and Marisa looked at him as if he had lost his wits.

'Are you sure?' Adam finished pulling his boots on. 'You didn't receive a knock on the head last night?'

'I know Brythnoth's cross is in the spinney. I want you to help me find it.' Ralph moved to the door. 'Are you coming or aren't you?'

'We're coming,' they chorused.

Adam wrapped on his war belt, picked up a small arbalest from the corner. 'Just in case some of our visitors from last night are hiding in the spinney, though I suspect they are now over the hills and miles away.'

Ralph tapped his own sword and dagger. 'We'll be safe enough. But don't tell anyone where we are going.'

A short while later they crossed the heathland, Ralph striding ahead, Adam and Marisa following behind. They had fallen silent as if they couldn't believe what Ralph had told them. They entered the spinney. Ralph paused and crouched near a corpse left lying in the gorse and brambles. The man was dressed in a brown leather jerkin, patched leggings. His boots and belt had been removed. A terrible gash to the side of his head had drenched his cold face in blood.

'One of the attackers from last night,' Ralph commented

getting to his feet. 'Dead and gone, there's little we can do for him. We'll tell Sir John and his corpse can be buried with the rest in the common grave.'

He entered the trees, pushing through the gorse, startling the birds which rose in flurries and cries of annoyance at this early-morning intrusion. The sun had risen but it was weak and watery, hidden by the mist hanging like a ghostly curtain over the flat Essex countryside. Ralph paused in the small clearing.

'Stay here,' he told Adam and Marisa.

He strode to the oak trees and stopped before the fifth in line from his left. He walked round its huge trunk, staring carefully up, but could see no crack, crevice or hollow. The hard bark was unbroken and even. If it wasn't this one, thought Ralph, it must be the fifth from his right.

'Adam! Marisa!' he called. 'Come over here!'

The two walked across.

'I believe Cerdic hid Brythnoth's cross in one of these oak trees. Remember the riddle he told the Danes? That he had hidden it in an altar sacred to his god and theirs?'

'The oak tree!' exclaimed Adam. 'Sacred to the ancient priests, while Christ died on the wood of the cross.'

Ralph clapped him on the shoulder. 'Exactly. We must search the trunk of each of these oaks very carefully.'

'Is this possible?' queried Marisa.

'Oak trees grow for centuries.' Ralph replied. 'These were probably here before Rome's legions left.' He shrugged. 'It's the only answer to the riddle I can come up with. If you think

I'm a madcap or wish to return to Ravenscroft . . .' He looked hard at Adam.

'No, no.' Adam smiled. 'Let's begin the search.'

Ralph waited until they were busy then walked across the clearing, straight to the fifth oak tree from his right. He stared up. On the side facing the glade there was nothing but on the other, just before the trunk branched out, he glimpsed a moss-covered hollow. He glanced over his shoulder. Adam and Marisa were busy searching. Ralph paused, whispered a short prayer then, using the knots and gnarls on the trunk, began to climb. After a while he managed to swing himself up above the hollow, ignoring the pain from the cut on his hand.

'Have you found anything?' Adam shouted.

'No,' Ralph lied. 'I thought there was a hollow but it's where a branch has been sawn off.'

He waited until his companions' attention was once more on their search, then drew the dagger from his belt – he had left his sword on the ground. He scraped away the moss and found quite a large hollow. It was full of fungi. He cleared this away too and put his hand in. Twigs, crumbling remains of acorn, the remnants of a bird's nest pricked his fingers and the hard wood scored his wrist. He leaned to his left, tightened his grip on the branch and dug his hand deeper. His fingers touched something cold and hard and what seemed to be bits of parchment or leather. He stretched in. The wood scraped his wrist, his fingers were bruised but at last he gripped then pulled the object up.

The cross had been wrapped in a leather sack which had rotted, and its silver chain was broken and tarnished, but the cross itself winked and gleamed in the early morning light as if it had been placed there the previous day. It was pure gold, six inches across, nine inches long, marked and scraped, but still a gorgeously rich ornament. Ralph stared at the glowing jewel in the centre where the crosspieces met and marvelled at the strange symbols cut into the gold by some long-dead craftsman.

'Brythnoth's cross!' Ralph whispered.

It weighed heavy in his hands, pure gold at least one inch thick. Bits of the leather sack still clung to the cross. Ralph closed his eyes, unaware of Adam's and Marisa's chatter, the sounds of the spinney. He felt as if he was stretching across the centuries, meeting Cerdic the squire who had hidden it here so many years ago. Ralph could imagine the young man hastening from the battlefield, desperate to return, wondering where to hide the cross. Perhaps he had played here as a boy and knew about this hollow . . . ?

'Ralph! Ralph! What have you there?'

Adam and Marisa were beneath the oak tree staring up at him. Marisa had picked up his sword and tossed it away. Adam's hand stretched up.

'You've found the cross, haven't you? You've found it! You knew where it was all the time. Pass it down!' The greed flared in Adam's eyes, his lips parted.

Ralph let the cross drop. Adam caught it and he and Marisa moved away. Ralph climbed down the tree and jumped to the ground. He picked up his sword then sat with his back to the tree.

'It's beautiful, isn't it?' he said.

Adam and Marisa came and knelt before him. Ralph noticed how Marisa rested the arbalest against her knee.

'It's magnificent.' Adam cradled it as if it was a child.

Ralph stretched out his hand. 'Let me have another look, Adam.'

Adam passed it over. Ralph held up the cross up and both the gold and the jewel caught the light, shimmering and glittering as he turned and twisted it.

'What will you do with it?' Marisa asked.

'I will look at it.' Ralph smiled. 'Then I shall travel to Canterbury. This belongs to the Church, it's a sacred relic. I am sure my Lord Archbishop will reward me well.'

'To Canterbury?' Adam was incredulous, eyes wide, face pale. 'You'll give this over to mumbling priests?' He leaned closer. 'It's treasure, Ralph. Take your dagger, gouge out the jewel, pay a forge to smelt the gold down.'

'Cerdic hid it here,' Ralph said as if he hadn't heard, 'because it is sacred. It was owned by a brave hero who was determined that it wouldn't fall into the hands of a pagan invader.' He put the cross on the grass beside him. 'We've been given this cross in trust, Adam. It's not for me or you.'

Adam narrowed his eyes. 'You knew where it was all o the time. Why did you bring us here?'

'Why, Adam, if I had left by myself you would have onl

followed. Better to have you sitting before me than an arrow in my back!'

'What do you mean?' Marisa snapped but her eyes shifted to the golden cross.

'Just look at you,' Ralph replied. 'Killers and thieves both, aren't you?' His hand fell to his dagger. 'You show no remorse, no sorrow. Your souls must be as dark as midnight, and to think both of you claim to be my friends!' He shook his head. 'You're nothing but assassins. You knew I was searching for the cross: it can't be mere legend if Ralph is pursuing it with such zeal, eh? And I was so trusting.' He balanced the cross in his hands. 'I wrote down my findings and I'd leave my manuscript on my table and my door unlocked. Who would care if Adam and Marisa, Ralph's bosom friends, were found in his chamber? I wonder how many times you visited. You must have read every word I wrote. And then that banquet, on May Day, when we all sat out on the green laughing and joking.' Ralph blinked back the tears and struggled to keep his voice calm.

Both Adam and Marisa were looking at him though even now they seemed more intent on the cross than anything else.

'I was truly stupid,' Ralph continued. 'I let slip that I'd find the cross sooner than later. You decided that I'd led you long enough. You could do without Ralph.' He picked up the cross and thrust it under Adam's face. 'That's when the darkness in you rose. A hurried discussion, was it? Old Ralph going up on the parapet walk but it wasn't me, was it? Poor Beatrice!

She went there and one or both of you brutally killed her. Adam and Marisa, the loving couple, who'd always be able to guarantee they knew where the other was when something terrible happened.'

'Ralph.' Adam shook his head but his hand had moved to the hilt of his dagger. 'You don't know what you're saying. You are overcome with grief.'

'What are you waiting for, Adam?' Ralph smiled back. 'Are you going to reassure me? Wait until I get up and turn my back on you? No, I'll stay here until my story's done!'

Chapter 5

'Not so long ago . . .' Ralph stared beyond these killers and was comforted to see some movement in the trees. He only hoped Sir John would follow his instructions and advice. So far, this precious pair had confessed to nothing.

'Not so long ago,' he repeated, 'we were just two clerks. Adam, you had Marisa, I had Beatrice. I mentioned Brythnoth's cross and what became an interest to you turned into obsession. You realised I was very close to discovering it. Why should I have the glory, not to mention the wealth? You or Marisa visited my chamber. Do you know, even before Beatrice died, I used to smell the perfume in my chamber but I thought it was a comforting trace of her presence. After you had killed her, I still caught the fragrance in my chamber, and also in the Salt Tower. At the time it reassured me. I believed Beatrice was beside me. Now I realise you used to go to my room, both before and after her death, to study my papers, to see what progress I was making.' He glanced at Marisa. She was very composed, head down, eyes watching from

227

underneath her brows, a smile on her lips as if relishing her own cunning.

'I was stupid. I really trusted you. Little Phoebe, she was different, wasn't she? Did she see you in my chamber? Did she overhear some conversation?'

'She was a meddling brat!' Marisa broke in. 'Ever at keyholes, or her ear pressed against the door!' She shook away Adam's warning hand. 'I couldn't abide her! Those clever eyes, that smirk, whatever she knew she'd trade for!'

'And you invited her to the Salt Tower to discuss matters, didn't you?' said Ralph. 'Then you killed her. She struggled. You beat Phoebe then you cut her throat. You wrapped her corpse in a canvas sheet and, under the cover of darkness, Adam lowered her body out of the window door and brought it here to Devil's Spinney. To all intents and purposes she had been attacked by some travelling chapman or tinker. You made one mistake: Fulk and Eleanora were hiding in the spinney. Fulk saw what you hid and followed you out. Perhaps he recognised you, your height, your build, your gait.'

'Oh, we glimpsed him.' Marisa pulled the hair away from her face. 'I was waiting for Adam in the Salt Tower by the window door. I saw the yokel trailing behind, pretending to be ever so clever. It was only a matter of time before he came back to bargain like the peasant he was!'

'And you'd be waiting for him, wouldn't you, Marisa? Just a few words. A pleasant smile, an invitation to the Salt Tower. Once he was there he was dead. Again, a blow to the head and his body is dumped in the moat. It might be discovered but his death would not be laid at your door. And Beatrice? One or both of you waited in the tower, watching that dark shape come along the parapet walk. Did you distract her? One blow to the head and that was enough; you made a dreadful mistake but you didn't really care.' Ralph fought hard to control his anger and grief. 'We all thought there was one assassin when there were two. Adam and Marisa ever ready to explain where the other was when these attacks took place. One of you was always seen or heard. Even the Constable was prepared to swear that he heard you checking the stores the afternoon Phoebe was killed but was it at the time of the attack? We don't know when exactly she died.'

Adam pulled a face and shook his head. 'I'm truly sorry—'

'Oh, spare me!' Ralph snarled. 'You're not sorry. You've lost your soul. All you can think of is gold and a life of plenty. You attacked me in the spinney, didn't you? Tried to make it look as if I had wandered into some mire. You are demons, both of you. You moved in and out of Ravenscroft with ease. Marisa would guard the window door in the Salt Tower while you, Adam, strong and able, ran across the heath. Once you were back in Ravenscroft you and your fellow devil could spin whatever lies you wanted.'

'We should kill him!' Marisa stared into the trees. 'Adam, we should finish it now!'

'Did Beardsmore suspect?' Ralph spoke in a rush. 'It was his death that made me begin to suspect there were two, not one murderer. I checked the castle armoury. No one had withdrawn arbalests. In truth you had two: while Adam loosed one, sweet Marisa would be loading the other.' He shook his fist. 'That day you nearly accounted for both of us.' Ralph gripped the cross as if it was a sword. 'And then we come to Eleanora, sly-eyed, quick-witted, Fulk's sweetheart. God only knows what she might tell Sir John and so she, too, had to be silenced. Now Eleanora was sharp-witted but when another woman came up to the small barred window of her cell and whispered encouragement, said she would do something to help and offered comfort, she believed her. That was you, wasn't it, Marisa? A piece of marchpane coated with poison for rats and Eleanora was no more.'

'Very sharp,' said Adam. He was slipping a bolt into the groove on the arbalest. 'I told Marisa, Ralph is keener-witted than you think. Likes to reflect, does old Ralph, tenacious as a fox terrier.'

'And you made mistakes,' Ralph taunted. He emphasised the points on his fingers. 'I gave Marisa Beatrice's perfume. I smelt that fragrance in my own chamber and in the Salt Tower. It would take two people for the assassin to be able to loose so many crossbow bolts at me and Beardsmore. You are a clerk, Adam, you would understand my cipher and writing. I was truly puzzled when I found that trap to break my neck in the Salt Tower. You, Adam, were talking to Sir John, but that left you free, Marisa, to go where you wanted. Somehow or other Adam quickly told you where I had gone. A marvellous opportunity! You could slip through the orchard, across that overgrown garden. You'd probably planned it beforehand, even left the twine from when you murdered Phoebe and Fulk, a warning signal should anyone come up to disturb you. You slipped in, re-tied the pieces of twine and were gone. If I'd discovered you, it would have been easy to drop the twine and act the concerned friend.' Ralph sighed. 'I was saved by sheer chance. I dropped my dagger and found the twine.' He paused, wondering if Sir John was aware of what was happening. Adam had yet to pull back the cord of the arbalest. Ralph held up the cross. 'All for this!'

'What are you going to do?' Adam asked softly. Both he and Marisa got to their feet.

'Before I left the castle, I left a message for Sir John to follow me.'

'He's lying!' Marisa spat out, only to whirl round at the crackling in the undergrowth on the far side of the grove.

Ralph lunged at Adam and sent him staggering back but he still grasped the arbalest. Sir John appeared from the trees, sword drawn, behind him the captain of the guard and a score of archers from the castle garrison. Adam's face broke into a snarl. He brought himself up on one knee and was trying to winch back the crossbow when an arrow took him full in the throat. Coughing and spluttering, he lurched to one side. Marisa ran past the oak trees. Despite her long gown and the shoes she wore, she was moving fast. Ralph put the cross down and followed in pursuit, ignoring the warning cries of Sir John. Like a shadow Marisa sped through the sun-dappled trees. She reached what looked like a clearing and hastened on. Ralph thought of the warning shouts of Sir John.

'Marisa, no!'

But she was already held fast in the mire. She struggled on. Ralph reached the edge and took off his war belt but Marisa had her back to him, floundering and splashing about. She was either unaware of his presence or chose to ignore it. She lunged forward as if she believed she could swim but the more she thrashed around, the deeper she sank. She turned in one desperate effort, her hand going up, but the mud was already filling her mouth. She spluttered and coughed, turned once more, and disappeared beneath the mire.

'She is gone.'

Ralph looked round. Sir John, chest heaving, sword gripped in his mailed fist, looked cold-eyed at the bubbles rippling the mire.

'She's gone. It has saved us a hanging.'

'And Adam?'

Sir John's fiery temper seemed to drain from him. He looked old and tired. He re-sheathed his sword and crouched down.

'I really liked him, Ralph, him and Marisa. I could have lived to the Second Doom and never suspected them. Ah well. Adam's gone. He was dead before he hit the ground.'

'And the cross?'

'My men have it.' Sir John plucked at a trailing briar. 'How did you know?'

'I could say deduction and reasoning, Sir John. But I suppose it was Father Aylred really. More a matter of grace than logic. He said something evil had come to Ravenscroft, not the ghosts or phantasms of Midnight Tower, but something else. I'll tell you later how they used that damnable door in the Salt Tower and covered for each other.' He smiled. 'In a sense, Beatrice helped. Marisa was so vain; she had to wear Beatrice's fragrance and I smelt it in places I shouldn't have. They are responsible for all the deaths. Only the good Lord knows how they will answer for their crimes to Him but answer they will.' He gestured at the marsh. 'Will you leave her corpse there?'

'I have no choice. The mire is as deep as Hell.' Sir John straightened and helped Ralph up. 'The royal commissioners arrived just as I left. I told them to wait. They look good men – a lawyer from the Inns of Court and a sharp-eyed knight, Sir Godfrey Evesden. Come on, lad.' Sir John clapped him on the shoulder. 'What you did was rather stupid, you know. Those two would have killed you without a second thought.'

Ralph shrugged. 'It was the only way, Sir John.'

They walked back towards the glade.

'Adam and Marisa would never have confessed or betrayed their greed until they had their hands on Brythnoth's cross. I discovered where it was, the rest I left in the hands of God. If I hadn't found it,' he spread his hands, 'who knows what would have happened.'

'The good Lord must have protected you.'

'Yes, and Beatrice. That cross, Sir John, was worn by a man who stood on the beaches of Essex and defended this shire against invaders. I do not think the angels of Heaven would have allowed two greedy malefactors to seize it so easily.'

They reached the glade. Adam's body had already been sheeted up. The soldiers were clustered round the captain of the guard, admiring the cross.

'And so what now, Ralph? Where will you go? What will you do?'

'It's almost the beginning of July. By the feast of St Mary Magdalene I will have left Ravenscroft.'

'And the cross?'

'On your goodness, Sir John, I would like an escort to Canterbury. I will hand it over to the Archbishop and pray in thanksgiving at the shrine of St Thomas à Becket.'

Sir John took the cross and ordered the archers to carry Adam's corpse and that of the dead peasant back to Ravenscroft. They stood and watched the soldiers leave. Ralph was aware of Devil's Spinney coming to life again. Only a pool of blood on the grass showed what had happened here. He stared across at the spot where he and Beatrice used to sit and felt a deep sadness. In his heart he knew a door had been bolted, locked and barred. Beatrice was gone. He would never come here again. He closed his eyes and said a quick prayer that Cerdic the squire would understand what he had done.

'I'll miss you, Ralph.' Sir John put the cross gently into his hands. 'It's true what the Scripture says: "The love of gold is the root of all evil".' He tapped the back of Ralph's hand. 'I can see this place has memories. I'll wait for you on the heathland.'

Ralph watched the old Constable go. He would miss Sir

John, Father Aylred and Theobald Vavasour. He vowed that he would spend the silver he had collected for his wedding day to feast them all before he left. He listened to a thrush singing its little heart out on the branches above him. He closed his eyes.

'Beatrice!' he whispered hoarsely. 'I loved you then, I love you now. I will love you always!'

Words Between the Pilgrims

The clerk picked up a jug and refilled his tankard. He hadn't drunk much; now his throat was dry and he wanted to hide the tears stinging his eyes. The prioress was staring across at the man of law whom she had known in a previous life. He just sat rocking slightly backwards and forwards. Sir Godfrey Evesden also chose to hide his expression behind a wine cup though, as he lowered it, they could see his glint of amusement.

'Isn't it strange?' Mine Host declared, nudging the customs officer, Geoffrey Chaucer, sitting beside him.

'What's strange?' Chaucer queried.

'How the pilgrims know each other.'

'Were you at Ravenscroft?' the summoner asked Sir Godfrey.

'Why, yes, sir, I was,' the knight replied. 'Both myself and the man of law, we were commissioned by his Grace the Regent.' He smiled across at the clerk. 'I only caught a fleeting glance of you. By the time we had set up our investigation and caught those responsible for the murder of Goodman Winthrop, you were long gone.'

'So this is true?' the wife of Bath squeaked, her cheeks bright with excitement. 'Oh, sir, tell us it's true!'

'But how can it be?' the pardoner asked. 'We tell tales from the point of view of the living. Surely this is just a fiction, a fable to keep us worried and anxious at the dead of night with the mists swirling about and the forest creatures crying.'

'What do you think, Sir Godfrey?' the monk lisped. 'I mean, sir, you did go to Ravenscroft.'

The knight gave him a cold-eyed stare.

'I was there too,' the man of law intervened, anxious to prevent a clash between these two old protagonists. 'I've spoken to Father Aylred and Theobald Vavasour the physician.'

'Sir.' The poor priest edged forward, his hands out. 'Why not say yea or nay to whether this is fable or not? Please!' His soft eyes pleaded with the clerk, who flushed slightly at the summoner sniggering behind his hand.

'I shall tell you,' he replied softly. 'But it is up to you whether you believe me or not.'

Chapter 6

Beatrice, full of curiosity, had followed Ralph from Ravenscroft that morning. She was pleased to see him returning to one of their old haunts in the company of Adam and Marisa. Nevertheless, when she looked behind her, she saw with horror that the Minstrel Man, with his ghastly steed and accompanied by Crispin and Clothilde, was trailing her. Moreover, the strange coppery light had taken on an eerie tinge and as Adam and Marisa walked, the early-morning sunlight turned their shadows a bloody red.

Brother Antony was sitting beneath an oak tree, hands joined as if in prayer.

'What is happening?' Beatrice called out.

'I don't know,' that strange man replied. 'But I sense the truth is about to be told. Beatrice, I beg you, stay near to Ralph. He is in great mortal danger.'

Beatrice watched her loved one play out his pantomime. She sat beside him, full of horror as the drama unfolded. She could not accept that Adam and Marisa were the cause of her death!

'Do you feel vengeful?' Brother Antony called out from where he still sat on the other side of the glade.

Beatrice looked at the gold cross in Ralph's hand. It shimmered in a special light. She studied the two assassins. She felt nothing but a deep sadness for what they had done and sensed that their souls were in a devastating wilderness where only lust and greed prowled like two wild animals. She, too, became aware of Sir John's men in the trees but was anxious lest Adam strike and help come too late. She was no longer concerned about herself. She kept moving in front of Ralph, willing, praying for his safety. She shouted for joy when the end came. She saw Adam fall, his throat pierced by an arrow. His soul had hardly left his body when those nightmare soldiers came tumbling out of the shadows to seize, bind then hustle him away. She followed Marisa's flight through the woods and saw her former friend sink into the mire, beyond help by any power on either side of death. Beatrice watched her soul break free of the mire and surge up, only to be taken by the demons it had housed, and then it was all over. Ralph talked to Sir John and, later, alone in the glade, whispered her name. Beatrice was also aware of other phenomena. Brother Antony was standing near, the silver discs of light had appeared round him, larger, more vibrant. Golden, dazzling spheres also moved backwards and forwards across the glade.

'What is happening?' she asked. 'Brother Antony, tell me!'

'The spirits of the just rejoice in what has been done,' he

replied with a smile. 'Brythnoth, Cerdic, all those linked to that precious relic, they rejoice and are glad. For them, the last tie which bound them to earthly matters is finished. Is it finished for you, Beatrice?'

She ignored him, running after Ralph and, though he did not know it, took him by the hand. Of the Minstrel Man, Crispin and Clothilde there was no sign. In the castle yard a knight accompanied by a man dressed in a fur-trimmed coat was busy showing documents to Sir John. She was tired of this place which had witnessed so much suffering. Ralph was leaving, the crisis was past. He had pledged his love for her and she for him. What more could be done? She wanted to journey on, to be free of all fear, to be with her parents and the others. Nevertheless, she followed Ralph as he trudged up the steps and wearily threw back the door to his chamber. He filled a goblet of wine, drank it quickly then lay down on the bed and stared up at the ceiling.

'Beatrice Arrowner!' Brother Antony had come into the chamber. 'It is time.'

She glanced back at the bed. Ralph was murmuring her name even as his eyelids grew heavy.

'I want to go on,' she said. 'But I want to say farewell.'

Brother Antony was beside her. 'I will go with you, Beatrice Arrowner.' His face had changed, no longer merry but smoother, younger, and his eyes had become a compelling light-blue.

'I haven't thanked you,' she said. 'Who are you really?'

'Why, Beatrice, I am your guardian angel.' He pointed to

the golden sunlight pouring through the shutters. 'Shall we go forward?'

'I would like to say farewell. Just one final word. I would like to tell him that I am safe.'

She expected Brother Antony to object but he grasped her hands.

'You fought the good fight, Beatrice Arrowner. You ran the race, you kept faith, so take your reward. Lie down on the bed, kiss Ralph again. Put your hands on each side of his head and go back to that very first moment when you fell from the parapet walk.' He walked towards the door and disappeared.

Ralph had turned on his side, eyelids fluttering. Beatrice lay down next to him. She stroked his hair and told him how much she loved him, how she'd miss him. The light pouring through the shuttered window had grown stronger, more dazzling. She felt an urgency for what had to be done.

'I love you, Ralph, I always will.' Her fingers were pressing against each side of his head. 'I will always wait for you; that has been my constant thought since I fell from the parapet walk.'

Ralph was aware that he was lying in his bed yet he did not wish to open his eyes. He was frightened that if he did, the very close presence of the woman he loved would leave him. He could hear her telling him of her love, sensed the urgency and the passion in the way she spoke. He was with her on the parapet walk. She was leaning down to pick something up and then they were falling. But, instead of waking, he was in the castle bailey standing next to her, looking down at her corpse on the cobbles. Sir John Grasse and others were running towards him. Nothing had changed except a strange, eerie, coppery light which seemed to suffuse everything.

'Listen and watch,' a voice urged, 'to what has happened in that other world alongside yours . . .'

Words Between the Pilgrims

The clerk of Oxford had finished his story and the pilgrims could see his distress. He would answer no more questions but lay down beside the fire and pulled his threadbare blanket up around him. The other pilgrims followed suit. It was not the most restful of nights. Strange, harsh sounds shattered the silence; there was a constant rustling in the undergrowth. The miller eventually got up and walked through the trees to the edge of the field they'd crossed. He came back to say they were bathed in moonlight but he was sure he'd glimpsed figures walking towards them. Many of the pilgrims drank a little more ale or wine and huddled closer to each other.

They passed the rest of the night untroubled and the sun rose in glorious splendour, dispelling their fears. The knight roused them, telling them that the next night they would stop at one of the most comfortable hostelries in the kingdom. Food was distributed – salted ham, watered ale and some bread they had bought from a villager's house. Horses and ponies were saddled, possessions collected and soon the pilgrims were streaming through the trees, back across the fields to the trackway, only too pleased to leave the woods.

The poor priest noticed the clerk of Oxford moved slowly as if reluctant to depart. Mine Host also delayed but the clerk was so dilatory that eventually the taverner shrugged and urged his horse after the rest. The poor priest, having sent his brother the ploughman ahead, helped the clerk to pack his most cherished possession, a tattered copy of Aristotle's *Metaphysics*.

'This brings back memories, doesn't it, sir?'

The clerk nodded. 'Devil's Spinney outside Ravenscroft is just the same.'

'And your story?' the poor priest asked.

'Every word is true, Father.' The clerk of Oxford, one foot in the stirrup, looked full at him. 'On the day Adam and Marisa died, I slipped into the dark. I dreamt, no, I saw visions of everything Beatrice had seen, heard and experienced.' He swung himself up into his saddle and stared down at the poor priest. 'I've been most privileged, Father. I have loved and I have been loved. Because of that love, I caught a glimpse of what happens after death.' He gathered up the reins. 'And, once that happens, what do you care about gold or treasure? Or preferment or benefices? We all have to make that journey, Father, and we must always be ready.'

'And Beatrice?'

'She has travelled on, into the golden light, Brother Antony with her. I can love no other woman. I would only see Beatrice's eyes and hear her voice. But come, Father, don't be sad. I wonder what tale awaits us this day.'

'Has your life really changed?' The priest caught at his bridle.

'Since that day of the vision, Father, the curtain which separates life and death has never been fully closed, even here. Last night I was aware of other presences.' He shook his head. 'But they did not concern me. We must be going.'

They left the trees, following the others down the slight incline. The clerk stopped. He looked over his shoulder and stared at the shadowy figures standing in the trees gazing out at him.

Headline hopes you have enjoyed A HAUNT OF MURDER, and invites you to sample MURDER IMPERIAL, Paul Doherty's new mystery of murder and intrigue in Ancient Rome, out now from Headline.

Prologue

'From one crime we learn the nature of them all.'

Virgil, *Aeneid*, II.65

Rome: Autumn, AD 311

The Tiber slithered sluggishly like a serpent along its banks, twisting and turning past the temples, the high-rise slums, the thronging quaysides and the gardens of the patricians. Night was falling yet the Tiber flowed and ebbed as it always had, peaceful now, no longer choked with the corpses which had floated and bobbed for days after the crushing of the last conspiracy. The Tiber was accustomed to such horrors: the blood-letting, the usual sequence following a mass proscription, gruesome murders and bone-chilling death. Along its banks Christians had been lashed to crosses, covered in oil, then used as human torches for wayfarers on the river. Now that was all in the past. Nero's statue on the Palatine Hill had disappeared. His great golden house, his palace with the revolving roof which displayed the constellations of the sky, all gone. Tyrant after tyrant had followed Nero, only to be swept away in the sea of blood they themselves had caused.

The criers now proclaimed a new Rome. In the catacombs beneath the city, the Christians no longer skulked, paying reverence to the bones of those who died before them in the amphitheatre of the Colosseum. All Rome was rejoicing. Constantine was preparing to march south and the usurper Maxentius was arming to meet him. What did it really matter? The Tiber flowed on. Thousands used it as a source of life: fishermen, merchants, traders and travellers. When the river ebbed, exposing the rich mud and silt, the poor of Rome, or the curious, would come out to search its banks for half-concealed treasures. The young woman and her witless brother were two of these. They came from a respectable home, or at least they used to. Now they stayed with their uncle, Polybius, self-styled entrepreneur, owner and manager of the She-Asses tavern. The young woman, Claudia, pulled the cloak her 'dear uncle' had filched off a guest from Ostia closer about her. She walked quietly, her sandalled feet squelching in the mud.

'Come on, Felix!' she called, then smiled.

Felix was wandering, hands dangling by his sides. He was not looking for treasure, but shells, the relics of life from the river. She ran back and shook him. His head came up, slack lips and empty eyes. He recognised his sister's face and, in the dim light, made out the signs her fingers made.

'You must keep up,' the message went. 'You should stay close to me. I've brought you here because you wanted to come.'

She stopped and half-listened to the noise from the city. Tomorrow she was to entertain her uncle's guests with a public recitation of Aesop's fables. Claudia turned away, Felix trotting behind her like a dog. They were so engrossed in their task that the man who stepped out of the shadows of the deserted quayside made them both start. Claudia couldn't make out his face, though his toga and sandals were costly. She glimpsed the chalice tattooed on his left wrist.

'Well, well, well!' he slurred. 'What have we here?'

He grasped her by the shoulders. Claudia fought back. She was used to such drunken attention, but now she panicked. The man was stronger than she thought. Felix came running up. He grasped the man's hand. The stranger threw him away. Claudia screamed. Her cry went unanswered. This part of the Tiber was near the Maxima Cloaca, where the sewers of the city debouched their waste from the latrines and cesspits. Felix closed again, his mouth open in a dumb scream. Claudia tried to prevent him. Her assailant moved like a viper. The knife he drew glittered in the moonlight, and with one quick slash he cut the young man's throat. Felix dropped like a stone. Claudia knelt down beside him, screaming, the tears flowing down her face. She heard a movement in the squelching mud. Felix's death had proved no obstacle: her assailant was above her, the knife coming down.

Rome: Spring, AD 313

She was beautiful enough. Her golden hair was decorated with a diadem. Pearls for earrings, a jewelled collar round her slim throat, its pendant hanging between swelling breasts. The circlet round her ankle was shimmering silver whilst the silk gown was cunningly dyed with purple. Her corpse lay sprawled beneath the black poplars in the Gardens of Sallust. Her pretty eyes were closed, the voluptuous mouth smudged with blood. The marks round her throat were still fresh. The angry red weals showed how her life had been throttled out. The assailant knelt down and checked the pulse in the young woman's throat and then, beneath the silk, the beat of her heart. All silent. The flesh was turning cold. The courtesan's head was turned, the golden hair pushed gently back. The dark-garbed attacker, balancing the knife carefully, etched the bloody cross, first on the forehead and then on each cheek.